BIG SWINGING D

WALL STREET ROYALS, BOOK 2

TARA SUE ME

AFTER SIX PUBLISHING

Me's series launch a must-read." **PUBLISHER WEEKLY on AMERICAN ASSHOLE**

ISBN ebook: 9781950017058

ISBN print: 9781950017065

Cover photo: Deposit Photos

Cover Design: Mister Sue Me

CHAPTER ONE

USUALLY WHEN ISAAC GREGORY'S control slipped at
work, he'd step outside of his Manhattan office
building, walk for a block or two, and return,
refreshed, and back on top of his game. Today,
though, he could walk to Brooklyn and it wouldn't
help. Matter of fact, if he made it that far, he'd keep
going.

He'd expected his first day in three years without
Lillian Bancroft as his personal assistant to be tough.
Likewise, he'd known she'd be impossible to replace.
However, if he'd had any idea how the first half of
today would go, he'd have called in sick.

Part of the blame was his. After all, Lillian had
given her resignation six weeks ago, leaving him
plenty of time to hire a replacement. But, in what he

could now admit was a delusional case of wishful thinking, he kept waiting for her to take it back.

Which was why he was on the phone seventy-two hours ago, desperate to find a temp able to start today while Lillian packed up her desk. And, okay, telling the owner and manager of the temp agency, "I don't care, just send whoever," was not one of his best moves, even when he added in the fact that it was then he realized Lillian was really leaving.

His concession on that point, however, in no way excused the temp the agency sent over this morning. Just thinking about the mess waiting for him back at the office made his head hurt. In less than three hours, the temp had "assisted" him by deleting two files of documents he needed for a ten o'clock meeting. Files she shouldn't have had access to, much less been able to delete. Then, because she didn't want to get in trouble for the deletion, had tried to fix it, and somehow, in a move that stumped his entire IT team, ended up encrypting another.

By the time she tip-toed to his desk at nine forty-five and, with tears in her eyes, whispered she was sorry, but she forgot to tell him his ten o'clock meeting had been moved up to nine, he was done. A quick phone call, and five minutes later, security escorted her from the building.

Unfortunately, not before he overheard her bemoaning to a group of administrative staff she never even got to see if his dick was really big or if the nickname was a misnomer. Fortunately, the rest of the staff knew his feelings toward that nickname and remained quiet.

He glanced at his watch and turned to head back to the office. He had a lot to do and no assistant to help. But on the upside, he couldn't see how his day could get worse.

MAGGIE WARREN WAS LATE. Which wasn't saying much, she was often late. But today, she was really, really late. She quickened her step, shifting the heavy load of compost while trying to look around the container to ensure her path was clear.

So far so good.

She hated being late.

She blamed the 'if only.'

If only her most favorite author ever, or one of them, hadn't released a book today. And if only she hadn't been browsing online and saw the email alerting her with a link to purchase. And if only she hadn't decided to buy it and read just one chapter.

Because who could stop at one chapter?

She knew she had to stop using 'if only' as an excuse to justify everything. But how could she when all the fun stuff was stuff she shouldn't be doing and the stuff she was supposed to be doing was boring as hell?

"Like taking compost to the collection site," she mumbled.

Not that taking the compost to the collection site was all that bad; it was what would happen after she dropped off the compost. Because that was when she had to look for a real job.

She didn't have to get a job, but after almost a year and a half of working here and there and filling in where necessary, she recognized she needed the stability. Plus, she longed to be in an office where she saw the same people day after day. To be around a group of people she could build relationships with. Maybe go out to lunch or something.

And one day when she was ready, like in five years, maybe she'd find a guy she wanted to have sex with.

God, she missed sex.

Now, however, was not the time to think about sex. Not when she was carrying a massive amount of compost. Sex and compost did not mix well. At least not in her world.

With each step she grew more and more aware of her hands getting slippery. Not to mention how the sun and heat worked together to make the compost smell even worse. She hadn't thought about how she'd desperately need a shower after carting compost. There was no way around it, job hunting would have to wait for another day.

Her favorite thrift shop was just ahead and while she wouldn't be able to go inside, the owner, Max, always had the most amazing window displays. She'd look at it closer on the way back home, for now she only wanted a peek.

Shifting the weight of the compost, she drew nearer to the window. Max must have gotten in the pieces from the estate sale he'd told her about last week. Once she dropped off the compost, she'd window shop a little and come back tomorrow.

That would be perfect. She'd stop by around noon and take Max to lunch. He had a habit of getting caught up in his work and forgetting to eat since his wife of fifty years died ten months ago.

She turned back around, making a note to call Max when she got back to her apartment.

"Mama, look!" a little boy who couldn't have been over five yelled and ran past her.

Maggie barely kept a grip on the compost, but she managed, and breathed a huge sigh of relief when it didn't tumble out of her arms.

What in the world had caused the little boy to run past her like that? She turned her head to see better, but no luck. Maybe if she moved over just a touch…

She hit something hard and unyielding. There would be no save this time. The container fell out of her arms. She watched in horror as it tipped over and the lid flew off. In a matter of seconds, compost covered the hard and unyielding thing, which she now saw was the most gorgeous man who ever walked on earth.

He just didn't smell all that great at the moment.

CHAPTER TWO

Isaac stared at the reeking sludge covering him. What the fuck? One second he'd been walking back to his office and the next, someone had dumped... what the hell was this shit?

"Oh, my God."

It took another second for it to register in his brain that the phrase was coming from the woman in front of him.

"I'm so sorry." She reached out as if to wipe the offending material off of him but shrank back. Then, seeming to think better of her actions, took a deep breath and starting wiping.

Fortunately or unfortunately, no one crowded around them or even stopped. No doubt keeping their distance due to the stench. So strong he almost gagged, the sharp smell made his eyes water.

The woman mumbled something under her breath. Though she helped in attempting to get as much of the stuff off of him as possible, she wouldn't meet his eyes.

"What is this crap?" Isaac asked.

"Compost." She picked what looked like a half-decayed leaf off his arm. "I wasn't watching where I was going and I slammed right into you. I'm so sorry," she repeated.

He watched her as they both worked to clean what they were able off. She was tiny for lack of a better word, no way did she stand above five feet two inches. Her hair was dirty blonde and curly. Not the fake curls women bought at the salon, but the natural kind its owner lamented about and tried in vain to straighten.

There was no way he could return to his office in his current shape, not until after a shower. Fuck, but he didn't want to get in his car. Not smelling the way he was. He'd never be able to get the odor out. He doubted anyone in the city would want him on public transportation, either. There was a shower in the gym he and Lance had added for their company.

Little good that would do since he didn't have clean clothes to put on after.

The only thing worse than a metaphorically shitty day was a literally shitty day.

"Technically," the woman said, "it's not shit. At least not the kind you're thinking about. You could probably stretch it and say it's vegetable shit, but that's not completely correct. Because they're decomposed as opposed to excrement."

He'd been unaware he'd spoken out loud. Even if he had, he wouldn't have expected a reply. Especially not one sounding more like a ramble than anything. He didn't reply. He didn't see the need to. Whoever this woman was seemed more than able to carry on an entire conversation by herself. She had thankfully moved on from the digestion of vegetables to compost storage and faulty lids and how she'd been meaning to get a new one and she would have made a better effort had she known this was going to happen. Again, Isaac didn't reply because obviously that ship had sailed.

She looked up at him, as if suddenly realizing she was the only contributor to the conversation. For a second, their gazes met and he couldn't look away. Her eyes were the most astonishing shade of green.

A green so vibrant he wondered if she wore contacts.

"Nothing else to do." The petite woman nodded and placed her hands on her hips, obviously decided about something, but he had no idea what. As much as she'd been rambling earlier, he couldn't believe she hadn't yammered on and on about whatever conclusion she'd just reached along with the path she'd taken to get there. "You'll have to come with me to my apartment. You can shower there and I should have some clothes that fit."

He didn't move for a long second. Surely he had heard wrong. There was no way a woman he didn't know just invited him to her apartment. When she didn't say anything further, he narrowed his eyes at her. "Have you lost every bit of sense you ever had or did you not have any to begin with?"

"What?"

"You heard me."

"It's my fault you're covered in this mess. I don't live far from here, and I have a shower and clean clothes." Those green eyes he'd been so caught up in moments ago, glared at him. "I'm trying to be nice."

"Maybe so, but it's a good way to get yourself killed."

"You aren't going to kill me." She lifted her chin, implying, he supposed, that was to be the final word on the subject.

"You don't know that. You don't know me. I could be anybody, and you're standing there asking me to come to your apartment." She still didn't seem to understand his concern, so he switched his protest. "How do I know you're not a petite serial killer, luring men into your apartment intending to kill them? Maybe the man who owns the clothes you offered is in on it with you and he's waiting even as we speak for you to bring in your next victim. "

"The clothes belonged to my husband." She spoke emotionless and dry.

Belonged. Did that mean he'd left her? On one hand it made sense. Maybe he got tired of the batshit crazy. Couldn't say he blamed him.

She took a step closer to him. "I know what you're thinking."

"Doubtful."

"I should have worded my sentence more clearly. The clothes belonged to my late husband, and no, before you ask, I didn't kill him."

He had not expected her to be a widow. Not as young as she was. When she spoke of her husband there had been a brief flash of grief in those captivating eyes, but it passed quickly. Isaac couldn't help but wonder how long he'd been gone.

Neither one of them could say anything because at that moment, one of the shop doors they were standing near opened.

"Maggie, girl." A frail looking older gentleman, stepped out onto the sidewalk. "I thought I heard your voice. What's going on out here?" He followed up his question with a glare toward Isaac.

"Max," the woman he now knew was Maggie replied and shook her head. "I knew you weren't eating the way you should. I'm coming by tomorrow and you're going to have lunch with me. Don't even think about saying no."

Max flashed Maggie a smile. "Only because it's you, but I promise I'm fine." He looked from her to Isaac. "Who's this?"

Isaac stuck out his hand since he knew Maggie couldn't answer and then remembered how gross his hand was. He pulled it back to his side. "Sorry, sir. I'm Isaac Gregory."

Maggie took a step forward. "I accidentally dumped my compost all over Mr. Gregory here and I've asked him to drop by my place to shower and change. We better be on our way before the smell gets worse. I'll call you in an hour to set up a time for lunch, okay?"

"You two go on," Max said with a wave. "I'll call and have the rest of this cleaned up."

"Come on," Maggie said, and Isaac found himself following her. She glanced over her shoulder at him. "Now you can't kill me because I have to call Max back in an hour and he's seen me with you. And you're safe because you gave him your name, and he's seen you with me."

"Maggie?"

"Yes."

"Turn around and watch where you're going so you don't run into anything else."

BY THE TIME they made it to her apartment, Isaac realized he should have asked Maggie her definition of "not far." He could have walked to his office and back twice by the time she stopped at her building.

He had to admit, if only to himself, it was not the neighborhood he'd envisioned her living in. Located near the Upper East Side, it wasn't one of the most expensive places to live in the city, but it wasn't the average middle class or upper middle class neighborhood, either.

A uniformed doorman greeted her with a warm smile but a wary eye at both Isaac's appearance and the surrounding odor. "Did you have a nice day, Mrs. Warren?" the doorman asked.

Maggie Warren. He assumed Warren was her married name.

"I did," Maggie replied all kinds of cheerfulness and unmasked enthusiasm. "Unfortunately, I ended up making a mess of Mr. Gregory here." She glanced Isaac's way with a smile and a wink. He didn't have to read minds to hear her unspoken 'Now two people know.'

Isaac couldn't say if the doorman replied back. While they waited for the elevator, he tried to remember why the name Warren sounded so familiar. On the surface, it shouldn't. Warren was a common enough last name.

A large party entered from what looked like a courtyard. The sign above the archway read, **Ellis Tobias Warren Memorial Garden.** He looked to the woman at his side who was completely oblivious to his revelation. No way.

He continued thinking as they stepped onto the elevator.

They stopped on the tenth floor and she led the way out. He knew the entire chrome and glass combination that made up her home didn't fit Maggie at all. And now he knew why.

Her father-in-law was Tobias Warren, the oil tycoon. His son, Ellis, must have been Maggie's husband. He vaguely remembered something about a house fire and the resulting death of the Warren Oil heir. But that was years ago. Was this the daughter-in-law Tobias's wife had publicly ridiculed and blamed for their son's death?

Maggie had reached her door and held it open, waiting for him to follow.

"If you go down that hall," she said, pointing. "The second door on the left is a guest bedroom with a private bath. I'll leave clothes on the bed for when you finish with your shower." She cocked her head. "Are you wanting to save that suit?"

He looked down. There was no need. He'd never wear it again, and it was unlikely anyone could get the smell out. "No, I don't think so."

"I'll pay you for it."

"Not necessary," he said.

"What if I insist?"

"I have a closetful at home, I promise I'm fine."

She nodded. "What size shoe do you wear?"

TARA SUE ME

"Maggie," he started. "There's no need."

"Eleven? You look like you're an eleven."

God help him. He only wanted a shower, and he was so close. "Yes."

"I think I may have a pair or two. Ellis was a ten and a half, but he was notorious for buying elevens." She headed down the opposite hall. "I'll look and see. If I have anything decent, I'll put them with the clothes."

"Maggie," he called and waited for her to turn around. "Thank you."

"You're welcome." A huge grin took over her face. "Be sure you close the door between the bedroom and the bath while you shower. I'll be coming in to drop off the clothes and the last thing I want to see is Mr. Happy."

Isaac felt almost human after his shower. True to her word, Maggie had laid out a pair of jeans and a tee-shirt. The jeans fit decent, but the shirt was too small. Isaac didn't care, though. They were both clean. She'd also placed what looked like brand new sneakers on the floor. He laced them up, glad they fit so well.

A quick glance out the window made him frown

and reach for his phone. What time was it? Surely it couldn't be as late as it looked.

Where was his phone? He pictured the last time he had it. It was still in his compost pants. He'd been so distracted when they'd arrived between craving a shower so badly and covering the shock that Maggie was actually part of the Warren Oil family, he'd forgotten to take his phone out of his pocket.

What he needed to do was to grab a cab and head home. He'd work for a few hours from there to make up for the time he'd lost today. And he needed to call Ty. It was his first day back and the man probably thought Isaac had abandoned him.

He stepped out of the bedroom, wanting to find Maggie and thank her once again before looking for his phone and heading out, when a crash from down the hall grabbed his attention. A slew of four-letter words followed.

"Maggie?" he called, headed toward the ruckus. "Are you okay?"

"It's nothing," she yelled from what had to be the kitchen. "Just a little cut!"

He swore under his breath. If her 'little cut' was anything like her home being 'not far,' she'd probably lost a finger.

The kitchen was easy to find. He followed the

sound of Maggie's, "Shit. Shit. Shit," until he stood in the doorway watching as she tried to wrap something around a finger on her right hand.

"Are you okay?" he asked again, but this time he watched as she answered.

"I will be." She shook her head, looking at him before continuing. "As soon as I can get this bleeding to stop."

He didn't wait for her to ask for help. With three long strides, he crossed the floor until he stood before her. "Give me your hand," he said and covered his surprise when she did. He was pleased to see she still had all ten of her fingers intact. But the middle one on her right hand had a nasty looking gash.

He took the cloth she'd been trying to use and wrapped it around her finger, gripping it and not allowing her to remove her finger from his grasp. "That cut looks deep, you should probably get it checked out."

"I'm fine."

Why did her answer not surprise him, even though her face had lost all its color and her voice sounded raspy? "You may need stitches," he said. "And unfortunately sewing people up isn't one of my talents."

"I'm not going to a hospital." She looked him

straight in the eyes as she spoke and though her face was still paler than he would have liked, her tone of voice suggested she would not take kindly to his insistence she needed to go to the ER.

"Then I'm going to stay here until I know the bleeding has stopped and you're not in danger of bleeding out."

"I'm not going to bleed out from that cut, get real. All it'll do is prevent me from giving you the bird." She tried to move her hand. "Let go of my finger."

"Not yet." He held on tighter. She didn't try to get him to let go, but the scowl she gave him told him exactly what she thought of his first aid skills. Too bad. She'd have to get over it. Although he hated to admit, the longer he stayed in her presence, the more captivating she became. He couldn't remember the last time someone other than his two business partners or Lillian argued with him. People generally just did what he asked.

"How did you cut yourself?" he asked. His assumption she'd been cooking appeared not to be the case. The counter was cluttered with all sorts of boxes and papers, but not one food item.

"I was opening that box." She nodded at a box near his elbow and it was only then he saw the large German forged knife at its side.

"You were trying to open a cardboard box with an eight inch chef's knife?" He had never met anyone who seemed as accident prone as Maggie Warren. Maybe the compost and knife incidents occurring on the same day were a coincidence, but he doubted that was the case.

"It's never been a problem before," she said as if that explained everything.

He bit back the words he wanted to say, reminding himself she was not his employee or his submissive, and he had no right to treat her as such. It didn't mean he had to agree or condone everything she did, he just needed to revise the way he went about handling a difference of opinion. "Now that it has become an issue, the next time you need to open a box, may I suggest scissors?"

She laughed at him. Fucking laughed. He smiled, not knowing at all what the joke was.

"May you suggest scissors?" She repeated, in a tone matching his. "That is so not what you really wanted to say, was it?"

"No," he admitted, both amused at her reaction and shocked at how much he wanted to make her laugh again. "But my other options were to open it for you, which I can't do since I'm applying pressure to your finger, or command you use scissors, but I'd be wasting my breath."

He'd said the last bit in a half joking manner, but Maggie didn't look amused. Not with the way she sucked in her breath and her eyes grew dark. Fucking hell. Did that mean what he thought it did?

"I bet you're good at it, aren't you?" she asked.

"Good at what?"

"Commanding people."

He kept his gaze steady on her. "I've yet to hear anyone complain."

"Will you let go of my finger now?"

"Only if you continue to apply pressure." At her nod, he let go and let her take over. He took a step back, trying to decide what he should do next. He didn't feel comfortable leaving her alone, but he'd stopped the bleeding and she was an adult, perfectly able to care for herself. Other than offering to open the box she'd attacked with the knife, and she might feel as if that was an invasion of privacy, there wasn't much else he could do.

He should leave now. Thank her for the use of the clothes, make a note to remind himself to wash and return them, then tell her goodbye, and get the hell out.

But he lingered another second.

"Will you stay for dinner?" she asked. "It's the least I can do after dumping compost all over you and then almost bleeding out on you."

He should say no. It would be the wisest course of action. "Yes."

CHAPTER THREE

Maggie almost giggled at the expression on Isaac's face after he agreed to stay for dinner. From what she could tell, he'd meant to turn her down, and it'd shocked the hell out of him when his mouth said otherwise. She refrained from laughing though, he'd put up with enough today because of her.

"Great," she said. "I'll make Chicken Marsala. I love to cook, but I don't do it very often because cooking for one sucks. By the way, I took your phone out of your pants, it's over near the sink."

She wished she could wiggle her finger, but feared she'd start bleeding again and bring on the wrath of Isaac Gregory. Although something in her belly grew warm and tingly at the thought of being on the receiving end of Isaac's wrath.

"Thank you," Isaac said. "Do you need any help?"

"No, but I'd really enjoy the company." Oddly enough, it was the truth. Sure she'd only noticed him crack a smile once the entire time they'd been together, but she sensed him to be a kind man. Somewhere under his cold exterior, beat the heart of a gentleman. He just needed to lighten up a bit. She watched as he took his phone, frowned at the display, and typed something.

Scratch that. He needed to lighten up a lot of bits.

"I'm probably not the best company," he admitted, sliding the phone into his pocket. "That's the case even on the best of days and today…." He shook his head, but didn't continue.

"Do you like Chicken Marsala?" she asked.

"Yes."

"Then stay for dinner and don't worry about keeping me company. Heaven knows I can talk enough for both of us."

That, at least, got half a grin out of him.

"See?" She teased. "You know I'm right."

She left him alone after that, not wanting to come on too strong. Heck, she didn't want to come on to him at all. Or at least that's what she told herself. When she'd stepped into the bathroom earlier to drop the clothes and shoes off for him, he'd been in the shower. He'd closed the door as requested, but she heard the water and it didn't take much imagination on her part to picture him. Especially since she'd had her hands on him earlier when attempting to get the compost off.

He worked out. Long and hard if her fingers were any judge. And though her fingers hadn't gone near the particular area, speaking of long and hard…

Stop it.

She needed to get her attention focused on something else. Anything else. She didn't have a stellar record with the opposite sex, late husband included. Only hours prior she'd told herself it'd more than likely be five years before she had sex again. That wouldn't change simply because she'd invited a sex god into her home.

She risked a glance at him. He had cleared a place to sit down in her dining nook and even managed to find the top of the table buried underneath all the paperwork she'd been avoiding. He definitely looked like a sex god, all blond and good looking hard muscles. For a brief second she allowed herself to imagine those muscles pressed against her as he took her roughly from behind.

"You better not come yet." His hand smacked her ass. *Hard. Commanding, of course.*

She moaned.

"Maggie?"

Her head shot up. She hadn't moaned out loud, had she? No, he looked at her funny but he had one of the papers from the table in his hand. She couldn't blame him for looking, not when they were all laid out before him.

"Yes," she said, wondering which of the papers had caught his attention: the information the insurance company finally sent two weeks ago? Perhaps the nasty letter she'd received three days ago from her mother-in-law?

"This is a stock certificate." He sounded shocked.

So was she, the stock certificates were the least interesting things on that table. "Yes."

"You have an entire pile here." He put down the one he'd been holding and picked up another. "And they're not all the same. I see at least three different companies."

"Yes," she said again, because of course she knew what they were. It was printed on them and in case she had somehow overlooked that fact, both of the much more interesting letters mentioned them.

"Maggie." He took a deep breath. "I work on Wall Street and these are quite valuable."

"Wall Street, huh?" She shook her head. "I screwed that up. Had you pegged as a lawyer."

"I'm serious. This is not an insignificant amount of money that, for all intents and purposes, you have scattered across your table."

"You think I don't know that?"

His gaze didn't waver. "To be honest, I'm at a loss trying to grasp what you know."

Her mouth dropped open.

"I mean it, on one hand you're this free spirit who carts compost and makes dates with lonely old men. On the other, you're the widow of an heir to an oil empire. I see you walking down the sidewalk of New York City carting compost and I can't make it fit together with the image of the woman who lives in this building. I can't figure you out for the life of me."

That she understood. "Imagine trying to live it, Mr. Gregory."

He at least had the decency to look abashed at his words. "I'm sorry," he said. "That was cruel and unkind, and I should not have said it."

"Even if it's true?"

"I've known you for a handful of hours. I have no right to make any kind of judgement concerning you."

"And yet if I heard you correctly a few seconds ago, it seems you have made several judgments about me." She held her hand up to stop any protests he might make. "And in many ways you were correct in your observations. I am a woman caught between two worlds. I have been for a long time. It's just gotten more difficult since Ellis died. He was always good at allowing me to be myself and shielding me from those who wanted me to be someone else."

"I didn't mean to make you feel or imply that you are in any way inferior."

If it had been anyone else, she'd have a difficult time believing them, but not only did Isaac sound genuine, he didn't strike her as the type to speak untruths. "I believe you," she told him. "I'm not sure why, but I do."

"Thank you."

She waved his thanks away. "I recognize I'm a free spirit or 'ho*pelessly unsettled and too unfocused to hold down a real job for longer than a week*' as my mother-in-law enjoys saying, but I actually had a plan today to try to do better. Or at least I did until I realized I smelled so bad it would be counterproductive to look for a job after carting around compost." She tilted her head. "You said you worked on Wall Street, what were you doing walking around?"

She wasn't sure why she asked. It wasn't any of her business and it'd serve her right for him to tell her that very thing. It didn't fit in with the rest of him, that he'd take off in the middle of the day to walk around the city.

He sighed. "I walk to clear my head. My personal assistant's last day was Friday, and I had a temp come in today to fill in before I find someone permanent for the job. It didn't go so well."

"I thought you executive types had the old person train the new one. Or at least that's what Ellis did. Unless the old one quit without giving notice."

"Not in this case. She gave notice, it was my fault, I didn't believe her."

"That's kind of dickish, don't you think? To act as if she told a joke instead of resigning?" But there again, Isaac didn't appear to be the type to do something so crass. There was more to it than that. "Maybe she quit because you were a jerk."

"I was," he agreed, surprising her. "I didn't know it at the time, but I was definitely a jerk."

"When I said that, I was joking." She felt bad now. "Like you said, I've only known you for a few hours, but you are nowhere near being a jerk. Trust me, I've

29

known several." He didn't look convinced. "Okay, tell me what you did that was so bad."

"Lillian was my PA," he said. "She worked for me for years following her divorce from Ty, who also happens to be one of my two partners. She didn't mind working for the company because we were opening an office in London and Ty moved there after the divorce to run it. But even if he hadn't, they talked all the time and got along great."

She raised an eyebrow because that didn't sound normal. "Really?"

Isaac nodded. "She often joked that they got along fine, they just didn't do marriage well. But not too long ago Ty said he wanted to come back to New York. Lance, my other partner, and I told him it didn't make sense to switch things up for no reason."

"If it's not broke, don't break it."

He snorted. "Something like that. But then Lance's girlfriend, who is a brilliant violinist, was offered a place in a touring symphony, based out of London."

"Ah," Maggie said, as the pieces started to fall into place. "So Lance and Ty switched."

Isaac shrugged. "We all thought it was fate."

"Except Lillian."

"Yes," his voice sounded pained. "She resigned as

soon as she heard he was coming back. Blindsided me. But I'd blindsided her first. I apologized. She would have none of it. She said he was a partner and if one of them had to leave, it needed to be her."

"She sounds smart."

"She is and the best damn PA in the business."

Maggie stepped away to get what she needed together for the chicken. "Best of luck to you finding a replacement."

He didn't say anything and when she looked up, he was watching her. "You mentioned looking for a job," he said. "Why?"

She shrugged. "It's stupid, I know, and won't change anything, but I want to prove my in-laws wrong." She kept to herself how lonely it was to be her at times.

"What kind of job?"

He'd said he worked on Wall Street, it made sense he would know people who had job openings. She didn't expect him to pull any strings for her, though. "I'm not picky and to be honest, I haven't given it much thought beyond how nice it would be to work in the same office instead of being shuffled around like I am with the temp jobs I take."

"You're with an agency?"

"I only work with a handful of companies. Those

who don't mind who I am." She'd never understood why there were companies who refused to work with her because she was a Warren.

"Doing what?"

"Mostly clerical. I used to help Ellis out. Planning. Stuff like that." She flashed him a smile. "Ellis and I were high school sweethearts, and we'd planned to get married after we graduated from college. I majored in Art History. Ellis told me I'd never have to work. I was young and naïve. Stupid really. I believed him."

"How would you like to be my new personal assistant?"

CHAPTER FOUR

THE NEXT MORNING, Isaac was still trying to decide what the fuck he'd been thinking when he offered Maggie his PA position. She'd agreed instantly. Of course she had. Almost as quickly as he'd asked her if she wanted it.

Hiring Maggie Warren was the epitome of bad ideas. Not only was she nowhere near being organized enough to function as his PA, but he'd thought about her all night. About her naked and on her knees before him, looking up at him with those green eyes that'd haunted him damn near every waking hour.

The only thing worse than hiring Maggie would be fucking her. He'd already screwed up and done the former, he would not, under any circumstances, do the later.

Yeah, you would, and you know it. Lance might live in London, but Isaac knew exactly what he would say if he was sitting in the room with him right now. Unfortunately, the Lance in his head was no easier to shut up than the one currently living in London.

"What's up?" Ty asked walking into his office. "After you disappeared yesterday, I feared me being back in New York was such a horrible thing, you decided to leave as well. Thank goodness you sent that text last night."

Once he finally made it back to his place, after a most delicious Chicken Marsala, he'd sent Ty a text apologizing and asking for a quick meeting before the staff arrived. He'd asked Maggie to come in around nine today. Normally, her day would start at seven, but he had several things to get into place before she showed up.

Ty took a seat at the round conference table Isaac had in his office. "Are we going to dial Lance in?"

Isaac wasn't in the frame of mind necessary to have a conversation with Lance about Maggie. Hell, he wasn't sure he was in the right frame of mind to talk with anyone about her, but it no longer mattered. In less than two hours she'd be here. "No, I don't see the need to fill Lance in on this just yet. I can send him an email later."

Isaac sat down across from Ty. Even though the three partners had gone to college together and had remained friends and business partners ever since, it had been a long time since he'd spent nearly every day with Ty. It didn't escape his attention that for the last number of years, he'd been closer to Lillian.

"I keep feeling as if I need to apologize," Ty said. "If it weren't for me coming back, Lillian would still be your PA and I know how hard she is to replace."

Based on the haunted look Ty had, Isaac assumed Ty was talking about more than just replacing her as a PA. Even though Lillian had worked as Ty's PA before the divorce, he was as easygoing as Lance and didn't have the difficulties Isaac had finding decent help.

"Funny you brought Lillian up. One reason I requested this meeting is to let you know I have a new PA starting today."

Ty nodded. "I heard the temp you brought in didn't make it until lunch yesterday."

Isaac cringed just thinking about her. "No, she didn't."

"Is the one today a temp?"

Isaac ran his hand through his hair, hoping it

didn't turn out that hiring Maggie had been a mistake. "No, this one isn't a temp."

"That was fast."

Isaac swallowed his laugh and the '*you don't know the half of it*' he wanted to say. "Yes. Do you know Tobias Warren?"

"The oil guy?"

"Yes, she's his daughter-in-law."

"Didn't I hear that his son had died? A fire or something?"

Isaac gave him a curt nod. "Yes, Maggie is a widow."

"Didn't I also hear that they suspected the daughter-in-law of starting the fire?" Ty leaned forward. "Are you sure she's the best one for the job?"

No, he wasn't sure at all that Maggie was the best person to be his PA, but it had nothing to do with the fire rumors. "She had nothing to do with the fire that killed her husband." Even if he'd thought it possible she did, a letter from their insurance company had been on her table along with those piles of stock certificates. The letter informed Maggie that following a lengthy investigation, arson had been ruled out as a cause for the fire, and it was their expert's opinion that the root cause was faulty wiring.

Also on the table was a letter to Maggie from her mother-in-law telling her they didn't care what the insurance company said, they held her responsible for both the fire and Ellis's death. Isaac had heard friends talk about how they didn't get along with their in-laws, but none of them sounded as bad as the Warrens.

"Have you already worked with IT to get her all set up and access to what she needs?" Ty asked.

"Yes, I took care of all that before you arrived."

Ty chuckled. "Have you been here since five?"

"Something like that." Five-fifteen, to be exact. "The other thing I wanted to discuss with you and the main reason I asked you to come in early, is that I was wondering if you were going to rejoin The Club since you're back in town?"

Ty and Isaac had been members of The Club since graduating from college. It was a private BDSM club with few people knowing of its existence. Members of the club were even fewer. Lance had never wanted to join, preferring to play at his house. Ty's membership, inactive since he'd been living in London, would be reactivated at his request.

Ty sucked in a breath. "Does she go?"

There was no need to ask which she he meant.

He only got the lost and haunted look in his eye when talking about his ex-wife.

"No," Isaac told him. "At least not that I've ever seen."

Ty nodded, but didn't ask any further questions. "I think," he said. "That I could handle almost anything other than seeing Lillian play with another Dom."

"She's not dating anyone I'm aware of." Isaac had probably kept her too busy for her to have much of a social life while she worked for him. He hadn't thought about it at the time, but she'd never said anything about all the hours he'd asked her to work. Would Maggie be the same? Was Maggie seeing anyone?

He didn't even try to pretend like he didn't care. He did and what was even more improbable to understand, was how he felt the need to protect her. From her in-laws and all those people who thought she'd had something to do with her husband's death. Maybe it was the Dominant in him.

"What made you bring up The Club?" Ty asked.

"I'm going to ask Maggie if she'll mind keeping up with my schedule there as well," Isaac told him. "Lillian always did and Maggie's a widow, so it's not like she's a virgin or anything. If you'd like, she could also keep up with yours."

"I think that sounds like a perfectly good way to get smacked with a sexual harassment lawsuit."

"It's not like I'm going to make it a condition of her employment, I'll ask if she would mind."

Ty leaned forward. "She's your employee, it's not enough to ask her if she'll mind. She could still say she felt coerced. Besides, just saying she's not a virgin isn't the same as saying she's kinky. She could be vanilla."

His partner had a point, but it had been so helpful when Lillian kept up with his entire schedule. Not only that, but when Maggie teased him the night before about liking to command people, he got the impression she wasn't totally vanilla. "Maybe I'll just say they're meetings after work I need her to keep up with. I'm sure I can word it in such a way that won't let on to exactly what it is I'm doing."

Ty looked at him for several long seconds before asking, "You like her, don't you?"

"It doesn't matter if I like her or not. Maggie and I could never be together."

"Why is that?"

Isaac swallowed a chuckle. "I'll let you see for yourself when you meet her."

* * *

MAGGIE HAD VASTLY UNDERESTIMATED the time she'd need to get ready for her new job. Part of that was because the humidity made her hair completely unmanageable. This was nothing new, she'd been living with her hair all her life, but for some reason it seemed to be different when she was getting ready for work. Damn curls wouldn't do a thing and she wanted so badly to make a good impression on her boss.

Isaac.

It still didn't seem real almost twelve hours after he'd asked her if she wanted to work for him.

It shouldn't matter what her hair looked like because there was no way she could look any worse than she did yesterday. And at least today she didn't stink. No, her hair shouldn't matter, but it did. She didn't want to give him one reason to regret his job offer.

She finally managed to tame her hair into a ponytail so it didn't look too much like she'd stuck her finger in an electric socket. Her entire closet was hopelessly outdated, but Isaac had wanted her to start today, so she'd have to make do with what she had for now. Maybe she'd be able to go shopping

BIG SWINGING D

over the weekend and find something more appropriate.

For today, she did the best she could with black slacks and a white dress shirt. Surely that would be generic enough to fit in anywhere. She checked her appearance one last time before walking to the subway.

Though she thought she'd left in plenty of time to reach her new office by nine, she soon realized she was cutting it close. The office was further away than the one she'd been working as a temp at and when she made it to the stop she needed to get off at, a quick glance at her watch told her she couldn't afford to stroll if she wanted to arrive on time.

She didn't jog because it would totally suck to show up sweating so much it looked as if she'd just hopped out of the shower; she power walked. Feeling accomplished as she neared the building, she slowed down. No need to arrive panting like she'd just won a race. Then it began to rain, and of course she didn't have an umbrella. With a sigh she spotted the office building just up ahead. She put her head down and quickened her step. At least with her hair in a ponytail it wouldn't turn into a ball of frizz.

She didn't slow down until she'd almost reached

the building. Was it her imagination or were people staring at her? It couldn't be her outfit. One out of every three females she passed wore the same black pants and white shirt. She glanced out of the side of her eye, glimpsing her head in a reflection. Nope. Couldn't be her hair. So far it was staying put right where it should.

Odd.

The air conditioner was definitely working inside the building. The drop in temperature paired with the faint sheen of sweat and rain on her body made her feel as if someone had dumped her in ice water. Nothing she could do about it, hopefully she'd dry soon.

Isaac had told her before he left the night before that he'd meet her on the twenty-fifth floor, right outside of the elevator. Nine o'clock straight up a glance at her watch informed her as she stepped inside. So much for being early, but at least she wasn't late.

She did her best not to sigh in impatience when the elevator slid to a stop on the tenth floor and even managed to smile at the guy waiting to get on. He looked up from his phone, took a step forward, saw her, and took a step, shaking his head.

What the actual fuck?

That had not been her imagination. She couldn't even pretend it to be so. The back of the elevator was metal. Not shiny enough to be a mirror, but if she turned the right direction, it was enough for her to see herself.

Or at least for her to tell that the rain had made her shirt and bra completely see-through.

CHAPTER FIVE

"OH, YEAH," Ty said as he waited with Isaac for Maggie to arrive. "This will never work. I thought it was a rule anyone working with you had to show up ten minutes early for everything?"

"Unspoken rule," Isaac said. "So she wouldn't know about it yet."

"I give her until Friday at noon. Or at least that was my bet in the office pool."

Isaac looked at his partner in disbelief. "There's an office pool?"

"Of course there is. I would have told you but I knew you'd want to enter and you can't because that would give you an unfair advantage."

"I wouldn't want to enter." Isaac was getting ready to tell his partner to grow up, but the elevator dinged. He looked over in time to see Maggie wrap her arms around her chest and step out.

She wasn't soaking wet, more like all over damp. He felt bad for her and wondered if Lillian had left any clothes behind.

"Good morning, Maggie," he said in greeting.

"Good morning, Mr. Gregory."

"Call me, Isaac. Everyone else does."

"I prefer Mr. Gregory."

He wasn't going to have an argument with her in front of Ty and everyone else to witness. They could deal with that topic later. He motioned to Ty. "This is Ty Bancroft, the other partner in the US at the moment. Ty, this is Maggie Warren, my PA."

"Pleasure to make your acquaintance, Maggie." Ty held out his hand, but Maggie didn't move her arms.

"Pleased to meet you, Mr. Bancroft," she said. "Sorry I can't shake your hand right now. I have a bit of a problem."

Ty put his hand down and raised an eyebrow. "Is the problem with your shirt or are your arms stuck like that?"

"Don't answer him. Honestly, Ty," Isaac couldn't believe his partner. He waved toward Maggie.

"Come with me, and I'll show you where your office is and we'll get you settled."

Or at least he hoped they could. She didn't drop her arms from around her chest, so he wasn't able to tell if she was injured or if there was something wrong with her shirt. He led her to the little office tucked just outside his own. He'd wanted to take her around the office and introduce her to a few people, but he didn't see how that was possible the way she refused to move her arms.

Unsure what to do with her, he stopped in the hallway outside of their connecting offices and pointed out his office, the nearest restroom, and the break room. He should let her sit and read the notes Lillian had left for her replacement.

"Isaac!" Someone called before he could open his mouth.

He turned. Nina, Lance's old admin who now helped all three partners, walked toward him. She held numerous folders in one hand and attempted to sort through them with the other.

"Yes, Nina?"

She drew to a stop before them, still juggling the folders. "Lance called. He asked me to print some numbers out and have you review them. He thinks they're wrong and the temp from yesterday somehow switched something."

"It's not the J and J account, is it?"

Nina grimaced. "I'm afraid so. Here you go." She pulled a folder out, and in the process, dropped three others. "Shit," she said, looking at the papers scattered all over the floor.

Lightning fast, Maggie bent down to help. Lance watched, amazed at how quickly she dropped her arms. He assumed whatever the issue had been, was no longer a concern. Until she straightened up, handed the files and papers to Nina, and turned to smile at him. Flashing him with the sight of her perfect breasts, encased in a wet white dress shirt and barely-there bra.

MAGGIE HAD NEVER BEEN MORE mortified than she was watching Isaac's gaze sweep over her outfit, and then his expression as he turned and walked into his office, closing the door behind him. Even though the damage was done, Maggie wrapped her arms back over her chest. She hadn't even made it through the first thirty minutes without wishing the floor would open and swallow her whole. That had to be a record.

Nina nodded in understanding. "That's why you were standing the way you were. I wasn't sure what was going on."

"It's raining," Maggie said while Nina picked up the last of the papers from the floor. "Or at least it was when I came in."

"And you didn't have an umbrella." Nina seemed to think for a second. "Come with me. I'll get you decent."

"Sure." Maggie glanced toward her office. "Let me drop my purse off and I'll be right back." The purse that from now on would always contain an umbrella.

Nina placed the folders she'd been carrying on a nearby table. "I'll wait here."

Much to Maggie's surprise, when she pulled the chair out from under her desk, she found both a clean, folded white dress shirt and a new umbrella. A glance told her the connecting door between her office and Isaac's remained closed, but somehow in the few minutes they'd been separated, he'd not only solved her current problem, but ensured she wouldn't have it again. She couldn't help but smile at how it made her feel warm inside to have someone look after her. Ellis had been the last person to do so.

She took the shirt and showed Nina, who looked vaguely surprised, but covered it well by asking if she knew where the restrooms were. Maggie nodded and Nina sent her on her way.

Five minutes later, she sat at her desk feeling much more human. While she'd been changing, Isaac must have entered her office again. This time he'd left a note explaining he was on a call and would come and get her when he finished. He'd left a binder for her to read. Notes, he said, from his previous PA.

Maggie read the binder from cover to cover, wishing the entire time the woman who wrote it, Lillian, was still around. The woman had a wickedly funny and sarcastic sense of humor. Maggie assumed Isaac had not read the binder prior to giving it to her. Surely if he had, he'd have removed the sections: THINGS TO DO BUT GIVE HIM A HARD TIME ABOUT and MY FAVORITE WAYS TO DRIVE HIM CRAZY.

Lillian had also typed a page simply entitled BSD. She explained it was a nickname people gave him, but no one ever called him the Big Swinging D to his face. Yes, he knew about it, but he didn't care for it, or Lillian added, that was always the impression she got.

Maggie read the last paragraph of the last page over and over, because it gave her the most insight into how people saw her new boss.

At the end of the day (which will no doubt be very late and well past working hours) Isaac is an absolute gentleman, but more than that, he is a good man. Exacting and perfectionist? Yes, and he expects everyone who does business with him to to be the same. Underneath his often imposing facade is a man who is compassionate and caring. He's also uptight and needs to smile more. Good luck with that one. I eventually gave up trying and instead worked to make everything run as smooth as possible for him.

Maggie didn't need the last page letter to tell her what a gentleman Isaac was. He'd proven that over and over in the two days she'd known him. How was it possible she'd only known him for two days? Surely it had been longer than that.

She closed the binder feeling uneasy. Not because of anything she read exactly, but because she feared her work wouldn't be up to his exacting standards.

He hadn't had any trouble firing the temp who'd messed everything up royally yesterday. If it ever came to that, she wasn't sure she could stand for Isaac to fire her.

She swallowed the lump in her throat at the thought.

She would make sure he never had a reason to let her go.

Besides, she'd much rather think about how he got a nickname referencing his dick. A giggle escaped before she could stop it.

"I should have known I needed to read Lillian's binder before giving it to anyone."

Maggie spun around at the sound of Isaac's voice. He'd opened the connecting door so quietly, she'd missed him entering.

He stood in the doorway between their offices with a confident stance and an air about him that bordered on fearless. She could have kept her eyes on his, they were captivating enough. Or she might have let the sight of his arms encased by the rich fabric of his suit hold her focus. But no, she'd been thinking about his dick seconds before and that's exactly where her eyes went.

And stayed there for the second or two it took to remember where she was and who he was. Her eyes snapped up to his, and if he had any idea about where her eyes had been, his expression revealed nothing.

"Thank you for the shirt," she said.

"Don't mention it." He walked further into her office. "Now I can talk to you without feeling the need to stop by HR after."

She felt her cheeks heat. "So sorry about that."

"It's not like you control the weather." He pulled a chair to her desk and sat down. "I see you found Lillian's binder. We have a few minutes before we have to be anywhere, I thought we could go over any questions you have."

Maggie breathed a sigh of relief and told herself she could do this. With renewed determination, she opened the binder to the first section she needed clarification on.

CHAPTER SIX

THE FOLLOWING days kept Maggie on her toes. There was so much to learn and she wanted to make sure she did everything correctly. Isaac had told her to be in the office at seven each morning. Because she wanted to beat him in, she showed up at six forty-five on her second day, surprised to see he was already there.

The next day she arrived at six thirty, and again he was there. She gave up, there was no way she could get to work any earlier, it would not happen.

"That's not even considered a morning person," she told Isaac when he informed her his typical day started at four thirty. "I don't think they have a name for whatever person does that."

"As long as you're here by seven," had been his only reply.

In the binder Lillian had written what kind of coffee Isaac liked best. Maggie made it a point on her way in on her fourth day to pick him up a large cup at a local coffee shop. Isaac seemed surprised, but he thanked her, and she continued to bring him coffee each day.

Just as she'd thought, she really enjoyed having a group of people to get to know. Everyone she'd met at the office had been nothing but polite, and she'd gone to lunch with several of the ladies. Isaac wasn't hard to work for contrary to what she had feared and what she'd heard.

During her first week, he'd mentioned he had some evening and nighttime appointments he needed her to keep track of. The first few, he would just send her in an email with notes of the different meeting times and people to meet. She marked them on his calendar and ensured he knew about them when the time came for him to attend.

Little by little, he transferred the PA duties to her instead of doing them himself. For the most part, she thought she was doing a fairly good job. He had never been late or unprepared for a meeting. And if her desk was just a little bit messier than anybody else's, okay, a lot messier, at least she got the job done.

Admittedly, Isaac gave her desk the side eye every time he came near it, but he never got on her about it or told her it was unprofessional. She appreciated that as none of her prior managers had ever kept quiet about the state of her working area.

Two weeks into the job, she thought she had almost everything under control. It was a Monday, and she smiled remembering the day before. She'd taken Max out to lunch and told him how she'd been able to keep everything running smoothly for Isaac. Though he didn't say anything, she had feeling Max didn't believe her. That was okay, she knew she could do it, what's more, she was doing it.

Isaac's office line rang, dragging her away from her thoughts. He was locked behind a closed door in a meeting with a client. A rather obnoxious client, from what she could tell.

"Isaac Gregory's office," she answered. "This is Maggie."

There was a sigh from the other end of the line. "I suppose since you answered, Isaac's unavailable?"

It was a male, and not a thrilled one at that. She put on her best happy voice. "Unfortunately, that is the case, may I help you with something?"

"Tell him John called, and I can't make our session at The Club tonight. If he can, I'd like to reschedule for Thursday evening. Whatever time he's able to meet will be fine."

She pulled up his Thursday schedule on her computer. "He has a few openings on Thursday night," she told John. "I'll check with him to confirm a time and then either he or I will call you back."

John gave a grunt and disconnected. Maggie drummed her fingernails on the desktop. That was the first time she ever spoken to one of Isaac's "evening clients" as she called them. Until now, he had been the one to talk with them. She'd tried to get information out of him last week about what those meetings were and who they were with. His answer had been vague, and the way he talked made her think he was teaching something. She'd asked if she needed to attend, but he'd been very clear with a quick 'no.' So clear, in fact, she hadn't brought up anything remotely connected to the meetings since.

'The club' John had called it. He had to cancel tonight's session at the club. On the surface it sounded like golfing at a country club. Except, who played golf in the dark?

It was weird Isaac was so secret about the after work meetings. Especially since nearly everything else about him was an open book. She decided to ask him about it once again after the obnoxious client left.

Thirty minutes later, he called her into his office. She walked in and waited while he finished typing on his laptop. She watched the top of his head and couldn't help wondering what his hair would feel like under her fingers.

"Thank goodness that's over with," he said, looking up. "Am I still free until two?"

She had checked his schedule not three seconds before. "Yes, sir, and the two o'clock is the only thing you have left on your schedule today."

He stretched his arms over his head. "A light day, wouldn't you say?"

"No, I don't believe I would, sir," she said. "You arrived in the office at five-thirty this morning, and if today is like every other day, you won't leave until six. The only reason you'll leave then is to make your seven o'clock meeting with John. However, he just called to cancel it and asked me to reschedule for Thursday. Which means you'll end up staying in the office until at least eight tonight."

"John called?" he asked. "Interesting. Put him down for Thursday. Seven o'clock is fine if I have that time open."

"You do." She almost didn't say anything else but hell, she'd never learn anything living like that. "What exactly should I put down, sir?"

He looked at her as if he didn't understand the question but he answered saying, "'John' at my seven o'clock spot is fine."

"But how will you know what you're supposed to do for... or with John?"

"I'll know," he said.

Yes, but I won't, she refrained from saying. "Why won't you tell me what it is?"

She wasn't sure why she was pushing so hard, it truly wasn't any of her business if he didn't want to tell her. And yet somehow she had a feeling she knew exactly what it was. Or, more to the point, she had a fantasy about what she thought it might be.

He sighed and ran a hand through his hair. A sure sign he was conflicted about something. "Did it ever occur to you I haven't told you because you might construe my words the wrong way?"

"I'm not sure I understand, sir."

"Then I'm not going to tell you about it," he said. "Do we have everything we need for the two o'clock meeting?"

"Yes, sir." He may have thought that was the end of the conversation, that all it took was a change of topic, but it didn't work that way. Not with her, though she would allow him to think so for a little while. The truth was, she would find out what the club was one way or another.

Five minutes later, she swallowed a groan at Isaac's insistence he needed her in the conference room for the two o'clock meeting. It wasn't because he asked her attend, it was so much worse. He asked her to take notes, and then type them up afterwards for distribution to all the parties present. It was the first time he'd asked her to take minutes, and it scared her. Or maybe scared was too strong of a word. She was slightly worried. But that wasn't quite right either, she was more than slightly worried.

She was worried. Her handwriting was atrocious. Sometimes she wasn't able to read it, much less anybody else. And if she couldn't read what she wrote, how could she possibly take notes and type them up later to give the people?

She had a feeling this could be bad. Really, really, bad.

Isaac found he could hardly keep his mind on the

meeting. Not because he wasn't interested, and not because it was after lunch, his belly was full, and he wanted a nap. It was because Maggie sat beside him and kept muttering something under her breath he couldn't quite catch.

He had been pleasantly surprised the last few weeks at how well she acclimated to the office. Yes, her desk was a sight, and he had no idea how she ever found anything on top of it. But she did, and that was the important thing.

Not once in the past two weeks had he been late or unprepared for a meeting. Maggie was a huge part of that success. After his recent failure with the temp, he had feared he'd find himself trying to send Ty back to London in order to beg Lillian to come back. Maggie, though different from Lillian in almost every way, certainly held her own.

In fact, the only downside to Maggie working for him, was that Maggie was working for him. Since she was his employee, he couldn't ask her out. Which was too bad, because he sensed a sadness in her that was at odds with her personality. He wasn't sure what kind of relationship she had with her late husband. To hear her talk, life was nothing but sunshine and roses, but people often said things like that to keep those around them from knowing the truth.

But none of that explained what Maggie's problem was today.

Finally, about forty-five minutes into the meeting, Isaac stopped for a ten minute break. Nina come in and showed the clients to the restrooms and the snack table Maggie had catered.

Maggie, didn't get up, but remained in her seat, mumbling and writing on her notepad as if still taking minutes.

"Maggie?" he asked.

Nothing but mumbles.

"Maggie?" He tried again.

"Just a minute please," she said, in a small voice that didn't sound like her at all. "I'm almost finished."

He peeked over her shoulder. "Almost finished with what?" She was still jotting down minutes from the meeting. How was that even possible? He looked around to make sure they were alone. No one was in the room except for the two of them. "Have you not taken minutes before? You don't have to write them, you know. You could type."

She put her pen down and looked at him with sad eyes that had no business being anywhere around her. It hit him square in the chest she was not as jovial as she normally was. "I'm a very slow typist." She sighed. "And I have taken minutes before, but I wanted to make sure I did everything exactly right for you. My handwriting's so bad I knew I wouldn't be able to read it later, so I tried to write slower, but then I got so far behind."

It didn't escape his attention that if it had been anyone other than Maggie, he'd be telling them to get themselves together and to do the job. But for some reason, it was different with Maggie and he couldn't stand the sight of her fearful and worried. He didn't know why and he didn't have the time at the moment to analyze it.

"You should have told me," he said. "I would have made other arrangements."

"I didn't want to disappoint you."

Voices sounded from the hallway. He made himself brush aside her comment for now and held out his hand. "Come with me. I need you to take care of something that just came up. I'll have Nina come in and take your place."

The smile she gave him touched him inside, hitting places he never imagined something as little as a smile could reach. He would go to extreme lengths to keep that smile on her face. There was no reason to even attempt to deny it.

They were at work, talking about work. Nothing in their conversation, actions, or surroundings gave the slightest hint of being sexual. And yet, he felt it. That something within her that had joked about how he issued commands, whether she knew it or acknowledged it, was present in the simple sentence she'd just spoken.

Maggie Warren was a submissive, and he was one fucked Dom.

CHAPTER SEVEN

THE NEXT DAY, Isaac had a lunch date scheduled regarding a charity benefit he had agreed to help with. Maggie thought she'd heard him say it was connected to Lance, though she wasn't sure how that was possible with him in London.

She'd arrived at the office with the expectation she'd go with him, but Isaac sent her a message around ten telling her he'd be leaving at eleven-thirty and not to expect him back until two. It wasn't that he didn't ask her to go with him that bothered her. She understood not wanting someone following you everywhere. What bothered her was he sent a message instead of walking the short distance to tell her in person.

Things between them had been odd since the

meeting the day before and she couldn't figure out why. She didn't think it had anything to do with the minutes. Isaac hadn't acted upset. Chances were it had nothing to do with her; she had a bad habit of assuming everything was her fault. Which sounded arrogant when she thought about it, believing she was so powerful and held such control over everybody that way.

With a sigh, she closed the spreadsheet she was working on for Isaac. She briefly considered calling one of the other admins and seeing if they wanted to go out for lunch, but decided she'd rather eat alone. There was a private patio off of the hall where the executive offices were and since she worked on the hall, she had a key.

She gathered her lunch and walked the short distance to the patio's entrance, breathing a sigh of relief at finding it empty. Though it was the middle of August, the overhang kept the area shady and relatively cool. Several large potted plants ensured privacy. She placed her peanut butter sandwich and the apple she brought from home on the table. A meager lunch, but it would do. She'd only taken one bite of her sandwich when the patio door opened.

"Hey, Maggie," Ty said. "I thought I'd have the place to myself. I assumed you'd be with Isaac."

"No," she said. "He went by himself today."

"In that case, mind if I join you?"

There was no way she'd say no to one of the company's partners. More than that, she didn't want to. Ty had only been nice to her, not to mention he was handsome and charming. He wasn't her type, but what did that matter if they were only having lunch? "Not at all. Pick a seat."

He sat across from her and pulled out what appeared to be leftovers of some sort. She wasn't sure if he cooked himself or if he hired someone to do it for him.

Ty looked up and caught her watching, but instead of the conversation growing awkward, he asked her if she was a sports fan. As it turned out, they both followed hockey, but Maggie was a hardcore Brooklyn fan while Ty pulled for Manhattan.

After several minutes of debating, when it became obvious neither would be swayed, Ty leaned back in his seat and asked, "How do you enjoy working for the Big D?"

His question caught her off-guard but only because she'd assumed if you didn't mention the nickname to Isaac, the same rule applied to his partners. Since that obviously wasn't the case, she replied, "I'm really enjoying working for him."

What she didn't add was to ask who wouldn't. He was smart, wickedly handsome, and to top it off, he was a gentleman. Sure, he was a control freak perfectionist but not in a bad way. He had never been cruel or disrespectful because someone didn't meet his expectations. People just seemed to naturally want to do their best for him.

Or at least she did.

"Can I ask you a question?" she asked Ty on a whim.

"Um...sure?"

"What's this club Isaac has meetings at in the evenings?"

Damn, but he could make his expression as unreadable as Isaac could. She did the only thing she could. She waited.

He finally gave a half chuckle. "Told you about that, did he?" He muttered something else under his breath, but she couldn't make out what.

"Not really," she confessed. "He only told me they were meetings. I didn't know about them being at a club until I took a call from a man who needed to change his session to another day."

Ty nodded. "And you want to know what kind of session?"

"What kind of club."

Ty leaned forward and caught her gaze. "What type of club might he belong to that he wouldn't feel comfortable telling you, his employee, about?"

A shiver ran through her, but she hoped she hid it from Ty. "I figured it had something to do with sex. Is he gay or bi?"

"What?"

"It was a man who cancelled, so it stands to reason..." She didn't continue, thinking it was fairly obvious where she was headed.

Ty shook his head. "It's not like that."

"Like what?"

"He's not gay or bi. Think about it, Maggie. What else could it possibly be? Does it involve sex? Maybe. Maybe not. What else?" He continued watching her. It wasn't sexual. It was intense. And it piqued her interest, but not down deep the way it would have if it'd been Isaac looking at her like that. Her eyes fluttered and closed. "You're thinking of him now, aren't you?" Ty asked.

"Yes," she answered, but didn't open her eyes. One, because she was a little embarrassed, and two, because if she kept them closed she could pretend it *was* Isaac looking at her like that.

"You're heading in the right direction," Ty's voice was melodic, she supposed it was due to the slight

71

accent he'd picked up living overseas. "Keep walking down that path and you'll find the answer you're looking for." A chair scraped on the cement. "I'm afraid I can't say anything else about it."

Maggie didn't exhale until the door behind her closed, signaling Ty had returned inside. She took several deep breaths even as her mind raced. Was Isaac a Dom? Was there anything else Ty could have meant other than Isaac's after-hours activities involved kink?

Even as she told herself it didn't matter because Isaac was her boss and there was no way she'd get involved with him, she couldn't stop the image in her head of him towering over her as he commanded her to strip.

A siren sounded from the streets below, preventing her from playing that fantasy out any further in her head. She collected her things, discarded her trash, and stopped by Ty's office before heading to her own.

His office door was cracked enough so those walking by could see him sitting at his desk. He lifted his head at her knock and smiled. "Yes?"

Maggie took a step into his office. The door was open, and she didn't want to blurt out what she was thinking so that anyone walking by could overhear.

"Um." She looked over her shoulder. The hallway was empty, but still…

"Close the door and come have a seat." He waved to the chairs in front of his desk. "If you feel comfortable doing so."

She closed the door and took a seat in one of the offered chairs. Ty didn't say anything further, and she saw no reason to beat around the bush. "I know you said you couldn't talk about it, but can you confirm if I'm right and Isaac is a Dom?"

Ty watched her for a long minute before answering. "Yes, he is." And something else clicked in her head as soon as he confirmed her suspicions.

"You are, too."

"Yes, but I haven't been active for a long time. Not since the divorce."

"Are you part of the same club?"

"Yes," he said. "Why?"

"I mentioned Isaac had a meeting Thursday night at the club?" At his nod, she continued. "Can you get me in?"

She never wanted to play poker with Ty. He covered any surprise he had at her bold request.

"I'm considered an inactive member," he finally answered.

Her heart sank. "And you don't want to change that?"

"I had planned to go by sometime soon and reactivate my membership." He kept his tone even so she couldn't get a feel for his thoughts.

"Can you do it before Thursday so I can get in with you then?"

He didn't reply immediately.

"Please?" She added.

He watched her for another long minute before replying. "I can stop by the club tomorrow and you can go with me as a guest. It'll get you in the door and allow you to observe. We'll set the goal of tomorrow to be making you as comfortable as possible in the space. Then on Thursday we'll return and you can watch Isaac. See if you're still interested."

"Interested in Isaac, or kink?"

"Either, both, whatever."

"It hardly seems fair to you," she couldn't stop herself from saying.

"Why is that?"

"I would think if you're reactivating a membership to a BDSM club, that you'd want to be an active part of the experience. Probably play with somebody." Maybe she shouldn't have said that last part.

She didn't want him to think she was offering to play with him.

But as it turned out, she didn't need to worry at all. He gave her a sad smile. "There's only one woman I want to play with, and from what I understand, she won't be there."

THE NEXT EVENING, Maggie waited for Ty in a café close to their office. It was her idea, because she didn't want Isaac to see them leaving together. Although for once, he had left before she did. It bugged her she didn't know where he was going. He had nothing on his calendar, and when he left, he'd only stuck his head in her office to tell her he'd see her the next day.

Either way, it was for the best. Maggie didn't want people in the office to see her and Ty together, either. That's how rumors started.

She'd never been to a BDSM club before and wasn't sure exactly what to wear. After a panicked text to Ty the night before, she went with a short black skirt and a halter top she hadn't worn in ages. It must have been the right thing to do because when Ty walked into the cafe and saw her, he nodded his approval.

"You look perfect Maggie," he said. "Are you ready?"

At her soft 'yes,' he led her outside and into a waiting car. It took awhile to get to the club, and when they pulled to a stop, the building was so nondescript, she'd never be able to find it on her own. She told Ty her thoughts, and he laughed and claimed that was the point.

It made sense. After all, when a place was named "The Club" the owners really weren't interested in drawing attention to themselves. But she kept that bit of information to herself.

They were let inside by a man so big and tall he could have knocked her down with his sneeze. Fortunately, he didn't suffer from any allergies and before she could have a decent chance to look around, Ty took her hand and led her toward an office down the hall.

He'd mentioned earlier he'd called the night before to let the management know they were coming. She saw why when they stepped into the office and were met by a woman not much taller than Maggie with multicolored streaks in her hair and paperwork ready for them to complete.

Maggie couldn't get her heart to stop pounding while she read over the information she'd been handed. The thought kept running through her head that she was really here. In a BDSM club. It was something she'd wanted to do for a long time, but she'd given up hope years ago, not long after marrying Ellis.

She shook her head. Ellis wasn't here now. She was, and that was the only thing that mattered. Not only was she here, but she would make the most out whatever time she had. Ellis was long gone, and though it wasn't her fault, she no longer had to live with his idea of 'normal' sex.

She had to stop thinking about her late husband. She'd loved him but he belonged in her past. He'd want her to move on. Although, she thought with a snort, she wasn't sure he'd want her to move on like this.

It took longer than she'd expected to finish her paperwork. Mostly because she took forever to get through the checklist. She put her pen down after finishing the last question and hoped she looked more calm, cool, and collected, and not so much, "People do THAT?"

At her side, Ty chuckled. Apparently, she hadn't pulled off the nonchalant look as well as she'd hoped.

"First time filling out a checklist?" he asked.

"That obvious?"

"Yes, but don't sweat it," he said. "Just think, the next time won't be near as scary."

"Next time." She nodded. "Sure, maybe in three or four years."

Ty laughed softly, and she couldn't help but do the same. Even though it had never been in her plans, she was glad she wasn't doing this alone. Ty, while not her type, was a good guy, calm, and even tempered. Not at all the way she'd pictured a Dom to be. But then again, Isaac didn't fit that mold either.

"Have you two finished?" The woman with the hair walked over to where they sat. "If you have, I'll take your paperwork. Since you're reactivating, Mr. Bancroft, we don't need to do a formal assessment. You can make use of the facilities today if you'd like."

"Thank you." He gathered his papers and Maggie's, stood up, and handed them to the club employee. "I think for tonight we'll only walk around, but we plan on returning tomorrow night."

"Very good, sir. Let me know if you would like to reserve a private room."

"No need for that," Maggie jumped in, not even giving Ty a chance to answer. "We're just friends." Although 'friends' might push it, she thought it better than saying he was an owner in the office where she worked.

"Come on, Maggie." Ty walked to the office door. "Let me show you around. I'm assuming not much has changed since I've been gone."

Maggie attempted to act as if she did this sort of thing every day, but the truth was, she still couldn't believe she was getting ready to enter a kink club. She fiddled with a loose string on her skirt pocket. Nervous energy, though why, she wasn't sure. She wasn't going to play tonight or anything.

"The women's dressing rooms are over there." Ty pointed out a set of dark wooden double doors. "The men's are further down and to the right."

Maggie nodded as she tried to take in everything. She was such a dork. They hadn't even made it into the main part of the club and she was already attempting to memorize everything she saw. To her left were a set of double doors, leading into the club.

Ty raised an eyebrow in her direction, and she nodded. Now or never.

He placed a hand on her upper back and opened the door with the other. Maggie took a deep breath, stepped into the room, and froze.

Though she hadn't known exactly what to expect, she'd thought she had a pretty good general idea of what she'd find on the other side of the doors. She could not have been more wrong.

The room they walked into was decorated with white furnishings and a white marble floor covered with soft rugs. Several of the couches were round and a fair number had people on them. Though members were in various stages of undress, other than submissives kneeling on the floor, there was no noticeable play. A bar was neatly tucked in one of the back corners.

"The welcome area," Ty said. "It's neutral."

"I'll say." She almost added that she'd never seen a room so devoid of color, but caught his meaning before she could embarrass herself. "I mean," she nodded toward the closest couch, "everyone is talking."

"This is also the only room drinks other than water are allowed," Ty said. "The bartenders are excellent."

"I might have to test that one out for myself in a minute." Maybe a drink would calm her nerves a bit.

"You're doing great." He assured her. "The hallway to the right is how you get to the private rooms. They're down a staircase. The public play areas are through those back doors by the bar." He glanced at her. "Maybe we'll sit in here and wait a few minutes before touring?"

"That would be great." Maggie all but plopped on a couch. "I could use a few minutes to convince myself I'm really here."

She'd expected Ty to laugh or at least sit down, but he remained standing, all the color drained from his face.

"Ty?" Maggie asked. "Are you okay?"

"Lillian," he said with a pained voice, eyes glued to the back door. "I think I saw her, and she just walked into the public play space."

His ex-wife? Here? Surely, Lillian hadn't seen them and assumed Ty was with Maggie. The very thought of it was ridiculous. But what if she did? Lillian didn't know her. Maggie could easily be someone Ty picked up for an evening of play.

Damn it.

"If you want to go after her," Maggie said. "I'm fine sitting here by myself."

"The hell you are," a stern voice said. She looked up to find a furious Isaac standing to the side of Ty. "And even if he thought about going after her, he's not going anywhere until he tells me why the fuck you're here with him."

CHAPTER EIGHT

"Excuse me?" Maggie asked, shocking the hell out of him, and standing up, fitting her small body between him and Ty. "If you want to know why I'm here, you can damn well ask me yourself. I don't need Ty to answer for me."

Isaac forced himself to take even breaths to calm down before speaking again. It's what he should have done before walking over, but one look at Maggie standing beside Ty and he'd jumped into his business partner's face with no thought beforehand.

Well, there had been a few thoughts floating around his brain. However, most of them had not been constructive at all. Most of the constructive ones dealt with how to dismember his business partner's worthless ass. Though Maggie had a point, he should listen to what she had to say before ripping into Ty.

"Fine," he said, though he didn't feel fine at all. "Tell me, Maggie why the hell are you here, and with Ty?"

She lifted her chin in that determined way she had about her. "Let him go after Lillian."

"Maggie," he said in warning, but she didn't budge.

"Let him go."

Isaac had fought enough battles to recognize one he'd never win. "Fine. Ty, go after Lillian, but if you break her heart again, your ass is mine."

Without waiting for Ty to leave, Maggie focused her attention back on Isaac. "You keep saying fine, but I don't think you are fine."

"How very astute." He wasn't fine. He hadn't been fine since an old friend and fellow Dom stopped him in the dressing room to say how nice it was to see Ty again and who was the lovely submissive with the curly hair with him tonight?

Isaac hadn't replied to the man. He'd spun around and made it to the lounge area as quickly as possible. His blood boiled with the first sight of Ty sitting in their BDSM club with Maggie of all people by his side.

"Did they have you fill out paperwork before you came in here?" he asked her.

"It was my understanding you weren't allowed in otherwise."

He nodded, but didn't add that Ty was known for getting around rules he didn't like. "I'd like to talk with you in a quieter environment. Will you go with me downstairs to a private room? To talk?"

"Just to talk?" she asked, and he knew he didn't imagine the longing in her eyes.

But even though he wanted to tell her the opposite, he replied with, "Yes. Just to talk."

She nodded.

"I need a verbal answer," he told her. "If you're going to enter a BDSM club, you can follow the rules, and one of them is all questions must be answered verbally."

"I didn't see that listed as a rule."

"It should be. But in this case, it's one of mine."

"Yes, Sir. Mr. Gregory. Sir. I will go with you downstairs to a private room."

Cheeky sub. She'd be a lot of fun to play with, but at the moment there were too many things in their way to think about that. "No need for the 'sir,'" he said.

She didn't reply, and he looked over his shoulder to make sure she followed. She did, but lagged behind a bit. No wonder. She looked this way and that, trying to take everything in. Her gaze met his and, hell yes, she was interested in this place. More than a little, if he had to guess.

She's not yours.

Yet.

He had to stop thinking like that. The first thing he needed to do was find an empty and appropriate room. The first empty room they passed was not appropriate. Decorated to fulfill any harem fantasy, the fluffy pillows and soft blankets scattered across the floor might be more of a temptation than he could resist.

The second empty room was set up like an office. Vetoed for obvious reasons. That left only one. Not his preference, but he could make do. Pushing the door open, he gave her what he hoped was a comforting smile. "This way, Ms. Warren. The doctor will see you now."

Her eyes widened, and she pushed past him. "No way. Really?"

Fucking hell, was she trying to kill him, because

he was almost there. He closed the door behind them and motioned for her to have a seat on the doctor's stool. There was one thing he needed to get out of the way before anything else was said or done.

"Are you interested in playing with Ty?" he asked.

"What?" She looked away from the stirrups on the nearby examination table. "No."

One of the tension knots in his back relaxed, but he wasn't in the clear yet. "Why are you here with him?"

"Yesterday, when you had that lunch meeting, I ate outside on the patio. Ty ended up out there as well, and we talked. I brought up the meetings you've had after hours and asked him if he knew where you were going."

"Did he tell you?" He couldn't see Ty breaking protocol like that, but he had to ask the question. After all, she was here.

"No," she said, with that smile trouble always seemed to follow. "He told me to figure it out myself. And I did. So I'm here." Her forehead wrinkled. "I have one question for you."

"Yes?" It surprised him she only had one, if asked, he'd have assumed she had at least a dozen.

"Who the hell named it The Club? I mean, seriously? That's the best they could come up with? The Club? It's the most unoriginal name, ever."

"I think that's the point."

"In that case, it's a stupid point." Her eyes flashed with something. "And why can't I call you 'sir' here?"

"That sounds an awful lot like a second question and you said you only had one."

"I forgot I had that one."

"Terms of address are personal. I prefer only a submissive I'm playing with call me, 'Sir.' Everyone else, including subs here, call me Mr. Gregory."

She took his answer in stride, neither arguing or asking anything else. Okay by him, he had plenty of questions for her.

"Have you been to a BDSM club or play party before?" he asked.

"No."

"Have you been in a power exchange relationship before?"

"No." Her answer was simple, but the look in her eyes was anything but. Whatever the look was for, he believed it dealt with something deeply rooted into her. But whether that was her doing or something someone else had drilled into her, he wasn't sure.

And unless she told him she would not discuss it, he wanted to dig a little deeper.

"Have you ever been in a power exchange scene? Topped or bottomed for someone?" he asked.

"No."

She had mentioned her and Ellis had been high school sweethearts. In that case, she probably didn't have a lot of experience, if any, with men before Ellis. And he would wager she didn't have a lot after his death either. Had her late husband not known about her interest in kink or had he been the one to suggest she repress it?

No matter what the answer to that particular question was, he had to tread softly. What he could not do was to pick apart or belittle her late husband. For better or worse, she had vowed to be with Ellis forever. That he died was unexpected and a heavy load for one so young.

"Why is that, Maggie?" He spoke in a low voice, hoping it would keep her calm and focused. "Why when it's obvious you're interested?"

She pressed her lips together so tight, he feared she wouldn't answer. A part of her wanted her answer to remain in the silence, that much was clear from the pained look on her face. His only hope was that the part of her wanting to talk about it was stronger than the part preferring silence.

"He said decent people didn't do that," she said in a whisper so low he had to strain his ears to hear.

Ellis, he assumed, but wasn't going to go there yet. "Did you believe him?"

"I wanted to, I mean, a wife should be able to believe what her husband says, right?"

It had been Ellis. Fucking hell. It would have been easier had it have been anyone else. But Maggie was no fool and had it been anyone else, she'd have been able to get past it herself.

"Should be," he agreed. "But husbands are only men. They aren't perfect and they do mess up and get things wrong on occasion."

"I felt bad for not believing him, but he left me with no other choice. If I said I believed him, that would mean I wasn't decent, and I am, aren't I?"

He wanted nothing more than to take her in his arms and tell her over and over until she believed it more than anything, how decent she was. Fists clenched tight, he fought to make his voice as calm as possible. "You're one of the most decent people I know."

She gave him a weak smile. "Thanks. I think you're pretty decent, too."

"Even though I have a membership at a BDSM club?"

"Yes," she said. "And no one would ever be able to make me think otherwise."

"Thank you, Maggie."

She looked away, but wasn't able to hide her expression or how his answer made her feel.

"Tell me, Maggie. What brought you here tonight?"

"I wanted to see if you were a Dom and if you were, if I….liked that."

After years of being curious, and not doing anything, he was the one who had given her the push to take action. Unaware and unintentional, but he had. He felt largely humbled. "By 'like' you mean, if seeing me as a Dom turned you on?"

Her cheeks flushed at his question. "Yes."

"And if it did? If you discovered you really liked me as a Dom, what did you plan to do then?"

"I hadn't planned it out that far in my brain."

Why was he not surprised? "The thing is, I'm your direct supervisor. It would be unethical of me to have any relationship with you."

"I know." She said, then a louder voice repeated, "I know, and it doesn't change anything."

He'd never found himself in this position before.

Never before had an employee interested him, much less a direct report. He didn't know what to do with it. Or did he have to do anything?

There was no reason to even bother answering that one. It was not in his nature to sit back and let things happen. To see a situation and not to do anything. Likewise, it wasn't in his nature to jump into something without first studying it first. He needed to do the same thing here.

"Maggie," he said, ensuring he had her attention before continuing. "Before we make decisions and change something that might not need changing in the first place, let's make sure we know what we're looking at. The session I have tomorrow night will be with John and his submissive. If you would like, I can talk to him and see if either of them would mind you observing. If they don't and you watch, you'll be able to see me as a Dom. Hopefully, by the end of the night, you'll have witnessed enough to tell if there's something you'd like to pursue, either with or without me."

Her cheeks flushed darker, but he was impressed as hell she didn't back down. "You'll be interacting with his submissive?"

"More than likely. Is that what you want to see, Maggie? My hands on another woman?"

"Not really," she admitted. "But if it's all I can have for now, I'll take it."

"What is it you want?" he asked, not sure if he wanted her to answer or not.

"I'll let you know tomorrow night, after your session."

CHAPTER NINE

MAGGIE FOUND it difficult to be still the next day. Granted, she was never one to let grass grow under her feet, but this was different. She wished she knew if Isaac felt anything but as normal, his expression was unreadable. In fact, to be around him wasn't much different than any other day. Rather infuriating if you asked her. But no one had.

She also wanted to check in with Ty to see how his night went, and to find out if he ever caught up with Lillian. But when she walked by his office door at ten thirty and he still wasn't in, she feared he'd called in sick because things didn't go well. Her hope was last night had gone better than expected and he was still wrapped up with Lillian.

She really hoped it was that last one. Just

thinking about it made her smile. The only problem with Ty not being in the office, however, was her getting into The Club. She wasn't a member so she couldn't get in by herself. The plan had been for her to go as Ty's guest, the way she had the previous day. She thought about bringing it up to Isaac but didn't.

That made her feel like a coward. And not just a coward but a stupid coward. It wouldn't be like she was telling him something he didn't know. He knew she wasn't a member and had no way to get in. He also knew it was his business partner that got her in the night before. Surely he saw the issue, he was a smart man. So why wouldn't she talk to him? She feared she knew the answer to that one.

She was afraid Isaac would see her as somehow less. In the same way she suspected Ellis had after she told him what she wanted to try in the bedroom. He never verbalized anything of the sort, but their sex life changed, after, and not in a good way either.

She didn't have to be told how ridiculous it was for her to think Isaac was anything like Ellis in that regard. Isaac was a club member for crying out loud. But the human mind was a mysterious thing. She could know her thoughts were ridiculous and still think them.

"Maggie."

Speak of the devil. "Isaac."

Somehow he'd managed to walk into her office without her hearing him. Fortunately she hadn't been drinking anything or else she'd be wearing it.

"Would it be possible for you to clear our schedules for Saturday?" he asked.

"Our schedules?" He'd told her to expect to work some weekends, and from the sound of it, this would be the first one.

"You and I have been invited by Lance's grandmother to lunch on Saturday." A faint smile played around his lips. "If I know the old bird, she has something up her sleeve."

"Why would your business partner's grandmother invite us to lunch?"

"Have you heard of Barbara Murphy?"

The name echoed in her mind. Something about it made her think she'd heard of the woman, but no matter how hard she tried, she couldn't remember when or where she'd heard or read the name. "The name seems familiar, but I can't recall why."

"She's well known in the fine arts world. She sits on several charity boards and oversees a scholarship in memory of her daughter."

"Ah." That explained it. More than likely she'd met the woman at one of her in-laws hoity-toity parties she felt obligated to attend while Ellis was alive. Since his death, she hadn't been invited to any event of theirs. Not that she cared because if they had, she'd have stayed home.

Isaac had been watching her, no doubt with his keen sense of observation, and picked up on her thoughts. "Mrs. Murphy is quite a character, I think you'll like her if you don't go to lunch with a preconceived idea of who she is."

She wanted to tell him it was too late but nodded instead and told him lunch on Saturday would be fine.

"I'll have a car pick you up at your place around eleven," he said. "Also, are you going home after work today?"

She searched his expression for any clue as to his thoughts on tonight, but came up empty. "I wasn't planning to," she said, trying to keep her voice as calm as his so he wouldn't have a clue how excited she was about tonight. "I brought my clothes to change into and planned on doing so there."

"In that case, I'll have a car waiting for you downstairs around six-thirty. Will that work for you?"

"Yes. Thank you."

"I'll be waiting outside for you." He dropped his voice, "We'll go over my expectations then."

What she should have asked him, she realized almost immediately after he left her office, was how the hell he expected her to get anything done after dropping those six words on her? Although to be fair, there were only two of the six words that made her insides flutter.

His expectations.

His expectations of her when she was his guest at his BDSM club. How was it possible those were the two most arousing words in the English language when said or thought together?

They really shouldn't turn her on the way they did. Hell, he really shouldn't turn her on the way he did. He was too uptight. Too controlling. Too much of a perfectionist. That he had the power to arouse her wasn't even logical.

Although she had to admit, logic had long left the building somewhere between compost and chicken marsala.

Logical or not, she made it through the afternoon and slipped into the backseat of the waiting car at six-thirty. A backpack containing the outfit she'd change into rested on her lap, and she drummed her fingers on it as the car crept into the nightmarish traffic of the city.

Was Isaac already there, waiting for her?

She didn't have to wait too long to find out. Even with the traffic, it felt as if she only had time to blink before the car pulled to a stop in front of the building she first saw the day before. And of course Isaac stood outside waiting for her. He'd said he would, why had she thought it possible he wouldn't?

Isaac walked to her side of the car and helped her out. "Let's step inside and talk," he said as the car pulled off. They walked to the entrance, and he held the door open for her. Although everything appeared the same as it had the day before, she felt different. Entering the building yesterday with TY had been exciting, but it wasn't the same as the almost nervous excitement she felt today, walking in with Isaac.

"Let me see what you brought to wear," he said, holding his hands out for her bag.

Interesting. Ty didn't seem to have been too concerned about what she wore yesterday. It might be possible to chalk it up to personality differences, but she didn't think that was the only reason.

He pulled out her set of denim short shorts and nodded. She'd got them for a Halloween party a few years ago and Ellis wouldn't let her out of the house because he could, "see her ass cheeks and she didn't even have to bend over." Isaac also approved of the thin white tank top she'd selected to wear with it. However, he told her to keep the heels she'd brought in the bag.

"You can go barefoot," he said.

"Why?"

"Because I said so." It wasn't the words he said so much as the way he said them. Even the tone of voice he used at work didn't seem as commanding, but she wondered if that was only her mind playing tricks on her. He continued, "There's been a change of plans tonight."

"Did John or his sub not want to be observed?" she asked.

"I knew I should have gone over my expectations first."

"What do you -" Her words were cut off by the finger he placed over her lips.

"Rule number one. You are not to speak unless I ask you a question or I ask for your opinion. You're not my sub, so while I can't punish you for disobedience, I can have you removed from the club.

"Rule number two. You will address me as 'Mr. Gregory.' You will not touch me unless I ask you to or give you permission.

"Rule number three. Anything I say goes. If you

become overwhelmed or upset or want to leave, you say 'red'. You've heard of safewords?"

"Yes, Mr. Gregory."

He smiled. "Very nice, Maggie. I somehow thought you'd be a quick learner."

She wasn't sure how it was possible for the excitement in her belly to both calm down and grow more intense at the same time. But if that was a result of him smiling, she never wanted him to stop.

"John didn't mind being observed, but his submissive, who is relatively new to the scene, did. She had some apprehension in general, so I've had another Dom step in who will be with them tonight."

So what would they be doing? It was on the tip of her tongue to ask, but according to his rules, it wasn't the time for questions.

"Come with me while I check us in and then you can go get dressed." He stood and held out his hand to help her up. Though he dropped it as soon as she stood, she didn't miss the jolt of electricity his touch seemed to send through her.

She felt calmer once she'd splashed cold water on her face and changed out of her street clothes. Plus, the overall buoyant mood of the dressing room helped. She knew none of the women present, but they were all friendly and inviting. Several spoke to her. Others, she could tell were shy or reserved. Whatever the case was, they all made her feel less nervous and teased each other like family. She stepped into the hallway where Isaac would be waiting with a smile.

He took his time looking over her from head to toe, and even though she was fully clothed, she felt naked under his gaze. Why even bother with clothes? She'd be perfectly content to strip and spend the entire evening naked. But then again, she'd never had a problem with nudity, either her own or someone else's, before.

"You look very nice, Maggie. Come with me." He held the door open and for the second day in a row, she stepped into what she now dubbed her white wonderland.

Isaac was nowhere near as social as Ty. Even though Ty hadn't spoken to many people the day before, he'd had a warm and friendly smile for everyone they came into contact with. It wasn't that Isaac was unkind or unfriendly, he wasn't as free with his emotions as Ty.

"We're still going to observe tonight," he said as they crossed the room without stopping. He pushed the doors open that led to the public play space and for a second, she stood and took it all in.

There was too much to take in: the people, their actions. Even more: the sounds, ranging from the rhythmic panting to grunts and moans. The pounding beat of the music coming through the speakers and the slap of leather against skin.

The room was a feast of offerings for every sense she had. If she stayed in one place, she could probably gorge herself. But Isaac wasn't about to let that happen, and she knew it without him saying or doing anything.

Within minutes of entering, he took her to a room off to one side and closed the door. He slowly turned to her. "Are you ready?"

CHAPTER TEN

"Yes, Mr. Gregory," she said, and he swore her eyes grew dark with desire.

He shouldn't be here with her like this. No good could come out of it. There was a reason he'd never dated an employee, and he knew better than to start now. Yet, he still couldn't find it in himself to walk away or tell her to go home. He swallowed a snort, like it'd do any good for him to tell her to go home. She'd more than likely smile at him and say, "No, thank you."

He couldn't tell her to go home tonight, so he'd have to find a way to give her what she was looking for while keeping as much distance between them as possible. Easier said than done, but acting more at ease than he felt, he stepped to the side so she could see into the room.

Set up like a mini theater, two love seats faced the curtain-covered back wall. Isaac checked the time. The couple they'd be watching had been alerted both when he opened the door and when he closed it. The plan was for him to raise the curtain after ten minutes. That would allow for him and Maggie to observe from behind a one-way mirror.

"Have a seat," he told Maggie and dimmed the lights before joining her. "We're going to watch a simple scene tonight. We'll be able to see, but not hear, the couple. To them we'll only appear as a mirror. You may talk freely while we're in here."

She leaned forward as if doing so would allow her to see through the curtains. "So it's like a police station? The mirror part, I mean. Not the rest."

"I'm not sure," he replied, while thinking it had to be a question only Maggie would ask. "I'm not sure, having never been in a police station."

"What? You've never seen an episode of Law and Order before?"

"Maggie," he said, bringing his finger to his lips. "Shh."

He raised the curtain. Maggie gasped and

dropped into her seat, eyes glued to the now visible couple.

He'd decided the night before to ask two of the club's staff members, one a professional sub, the other a professional Dom, to run a scene for observation. He'd spoken with the Dom about a few things but mostly, left everything up to the pro. Isaac bit back a laugh because a police station had been selected for the setting.

The female sub was naked and bent over a desk, her wrists were handcuffed together, but she did not appear bound to the desk. Her red hair had been tied into a ponytail which showed part of her expression since they were positioned with profiles facing the mirror.

Behind her and off to the side, the Dom stood so she could not see him if she turned to look in the mirror. A quick glance to his side showed Maggie was enthralled with the scene before her. She sat to one side of the love seat, her arm along one of the arm rests. To look at the overall picture she made, one would think she was relaxed. However, the white-knuckle grip she had on the end of the arm rest shot that theory straight to hell.

He had not chosen to sit next to her originally, but as the couple began their play, he stood and not making a sound, sat down next to her. He draped his arm across the back of the love seat. Being this close to Maggie, he felt a tremor of excitement as the Dom before them walked to the submissive's side, dragging his hand across her ass and giving it a hard smack.

"There are many ways to bind a submissive," Isaac said. "The one we see now has handcuffs on, but there's more. What is it that keeps her bound to the desk?"

"Sir?" Maggie asked, not moving an inch, clearly not wanting to look away from the scene for a second.

He leaned close and whispered in her ear, "Why doesn't she move? She can. Why does she stay when she has the freedom to stand up and leave?"

There was no right or wrong answer. His hope was Maggie saw herself in the submissive's spot. That in her mind, she was the one in handcuffs and bent over a desk. Because if she did, her answer would probably be why Maggie stayed.

And he wanted to know her why.

He didn't fool himself into thinking it was because she was new to actual play and her reply would answer some intellectual hypothesis. No, if she pictured herself as the submissive, it was possible she saw him as the Dom. And he wanted to know why Maggie would stay where she was when he was prepared to use her.

"Maggie?" he urged her. "Tell me."

She ran the tip of her tongue across her lips. "Him," she said in a breathy voice. "She stays because he told her to get in that position and she'll stay there until he tells her to move or else he picks her up and moves her himself."

He gave a hum of approval. "Very nice, Maggie." He brushed a finger along her nape and delighted in her shiver. "Why does she do what he tells her? She's a grown woman, probably has a full-time job, why should she do something just because a man tells her?"

Maggie didn't even stop to think about her answer. "Because in this moment, he's not just a man. He's her Master. She has nothing to give him that is worthy enough to show him what he means to her, what he does to her, how he makes her feel. So, she gives him the most precious thing she has." Maggie lifted her shoulders in a small shrug, as if to say, it was nothing, but in fact, it was everything. "She gives him herself."

Although he had told himself there was no right or wrong answer, he wasn't sure anyone could reply with anything more perfect than what she said.

"Maggie," he whispered.

This time she turned away from watching the couple and when her eyes found his, they were searching. He didn't know what for, he doubted she knew, but when she leaned forward ever so slightly and whispered, "Mr. Gregory," everything other than her blurred.

He brushed a few wayward curls out of her eyes, allowing his fingers to linger longer than necessary along her cheekbone. God help him, he'd known if he touched her once, he'd want more. He searched her expression, but found no trace of hesitation or uncertainty. Slipping his fingers through her hair, he pulled her close. "What am I going to do with you?"

Her eyes sparkled. He'd always heard that expression and thought it didn't make a bit of sense. But now he knew that was because he'd never known anyone filled with so much joy it simply had no choice but to naturally radiate from them.

"I'm hoping you'll kiss me," she whispered.

It was the best damn idea he believed he'd ever heard. Shoving aside every alarm and every voice in his head telling him all the reasons why he shouldn't, he closed the distance between them and grazed his lips across hers.

Maggie, however, clearly wanted nothing to do with grazing. The second he lifted his head, she murmured, "Let me touch you."

"Yes." It slipped from his lips effortlessly and without thought, other than the thought about how he desperately wanted her hands on him.

At first she was tentative and unsure, but he shifted so she felt his length, hard and straining against the confines of his pants. "That's what you do to me," he said. "How your touch makes me react."

His words made her bold. Her touches were no longer hesitant. With what felt like renewed and excited energy she tugged at his shirt, trying to pull it loose. Somewhere between her hand sneaking into his waistband and the unexpected gasp she gave when he nibbled the side of her neck, he made himself push away.

Maggie whimpered and attempted to pull him back. It would be so easy to allow it, to just give in, and let what happened to happen. But Isaac couldn't afford it. Not professionally by going too far with an employee and not here at the club where he was too highly regarded to forget himself over a few sweet kisses and touches he'd already decided shouldn't happen.

"We're missing the scene." He pulled her to his side, wrapping his arms around her and holding her close, not caring if he should or not. He wouldn't allow himself to kiss her again, but he'd be damned if he'd keep his hands off her. She snuggled into him and sighed, a picture of utter contentment.

Before them the scene played on, the couple on the other side of the glass unaware they'd been ignored for the last ten or so minutes. The Dom had blindfolded his sub and was spanking her with a wicked looking paddle.

"Do you enjoy being spanked, Maggie?" Isaac asked. "To be bent over with your bare ass up in the air waiting for your Dom to redden it? Waiting for the feel of his hand to strike your flesh? Wanting it so bad and yet not sure because you know it'll hurt? And even that doesn't make you want to leave, does it? Why is that?"

"Because I want them both," Maggie said, her focus on the woman on the other side of the glass writhing under the hand of her Dom. "I want the pain and the pleasure and I want to feel how hard you get while you're using me like that. And then when you finish I want to kneel before you and take your cock in my mouth so I can suck you and make you come in my mouth. You hold my mouth closed to ensure I swallow everything you gave me. I can't tell you at that moment because my mouth is full but you don't have to do that. There's nothing I want more than to show you with my mouth how wonderful you make me feel and that includes swallowing."

Holy hell, he had not anticipated Maggie having a dirty mouth, and it turned him on more than he already was, which he wouldn't have thought possible ten minutes ago.

"Is that a spreader bar?" Maggie asked, with a nod toward the couple.

The Dom had placed the paddle on the desk and now carried a spreader bar. He left it on the ground near her feet, ran his hand over a reddened butt cheek, and said something that had his sub shaking her head.

"Yes," Isaac confirmed. "I happen to like them as well. Very useful to have on hand when a sub is a bit shy about being spread wide. Is that something you would enjoy being used on you?"

She indicated it was, and he made a note to have her fill out a checklist for him. She'd filled one out for the club, it was a standing rule that one had to be in place before a person could enter, but he wanted her to do a separate one for him.

Beside him, Maggie's breath hitched slightly, eyes still locked on the couple. Isaac looked that way and saw the Dom had lubed his cock and had it in hand, easing it gently into the sub's ass.

"Have you ever had anal sex, Maggie?" he asked.

"No, Mr. Gregory," she said but couldn't tear her gaze from the scene. "Ellis said it was unnatural. But I've always wanted to try it. At least once."

Part of Isaac wished Ellis was still around so he could ask him what his deal was and why he refused to at least try some fantasies Maggie had. Then again, on second thought, it was better this way. Ellis's loss was Isaac's gain. He had no problem helping Maggie explore her sexuality.

Or he wouldn't if he hadn't been so damn quick to offer her a job.

CHAPTER ELEVEN

As SHE WAITED for Isaac to pick her up the next day, Maggie wished she hadn't taken the assistant job. From what she could tell, as long as she worked for him, Isaac wouldn't go any further than the kiss they'd shared the night before. And frankly, that sucked hairy balls because that kiss had been amazing. If a simple kiss had been so great, thinking about how amazing everything else would be with Isaac sent her mind spinning with naughty fantasies.

She'd enjoyed watching the couple play at the club the night before. And though Isaac had asked her a few questions when it was over, he made it clear he didn't play with employees. She gave more than a minute's thought to quitting but decided against doing so. No need to give the in-laws more ammunition to use against her. For now, her naughty fantasies would have to stay just that.

Five minutes before he was due to arrive, she made her way down to the lobby. If she'd learned anything about Isaac, she'd learned he was always early to everything. Somehow, she wasn't surprised to find him already outside, waiting.

Once he spotted her, he hopped out of the car and walked around to open the passenger side for her.

"Thank you," she said calmly, or at least as calm as possible when he was standing there looking like sex personified. He wore a light tan suit, but no tie. The shirt he wore didn't have the top buttons fastened. Not to mention its blue hue brought out the color in his eyes, making them somehow bluer than normal. This casual, weekend Isaac would be the one that made her slip up and mention how much she wanted to do nasty filthy things with him.

"Are we going to Lance's grandmother's house?" she asked as Isaac headed out of the city. When she called her that instead of Barbara Murphy she could pretend in her head the woman could be anyone and not more than likely a friend of her in-laws.

"Yes," Isaac said. "Lance lived with her part time before he moved to London and the scholarship students do as well. I don't think any of them are living at the estate at the moment, though."

Which made sense in her mind. If she was a scholarship student, she wouldn't want to live with someone like the Warrens who would forever hold it over their heads they were only where they were because of charity.

Her stomach churned. She prayed she didn't vomit all over the interior of Isaac's car. God, she hated rich, snotty people.

In no time at all, they pulled into a pretentious driveway she knew would lead to an equally pretentious house. Although 'house' would be a grievous insult to the obscene monstrosity she knew without a doubt would be at the end of the driveway.

And she knew because her in-laws lived no more than five miles away.

"Are you okay?" Isaac asked. "You look a bit green."

"I'm fine," she said, deciding his word from a few days ago fit her mood perfectly. His expression said he didn't believe her, but he didn't verbalize his thoughts.

As expected, the house was every bit as grand and showy as she'd pictured. She took a deep breath as Isaac opened her door and helped her out.

"No," he said, placing a hand on the small of her back and leading her up the walkway to the house. "You're not fine. Not at the moment."

"Yeah," she said in a half snort. "I'll be fine when I get to leave this place."

They came to a stop at the front door. He dropped his head to her ear and whispered, "Trust me."

The warmth of his breath against her skin made her shiver. She wanted more than anything to believe him. But how could she when so much of her life experience had ensured she knew exactly the type of woman who lived behind that door?

And what would happen when she turned out to be right? Who would shield her? Ellis had always kept his parents from doing their worst to her. She didn't know Isaac well enough to expect him to do the same. Especially when it was the grandparent of a business partner. She didn't need anyone to tell her who Isaac would choose if he had to pick between her and Mrs. Barbara Murphy.

But he was looking down at her with such a look of expectation, she couldn't tell him no. She gave him the best she could give at the moment. "I'll try." It wasn't enough, and she knew it, but it was all she had.

The front door flew open with an "Isaac!" that made her nearly jump out of her skin. It took a second for her to realize the sound came from an older woman, standing in the now open doorway.

At first glance, she looked like all the other wealthy socialites over sixty Maggie had ever met. Perfectly coiffed hair. Expertly tailored designer suit. Sensible shoes. The only thing missing was the string of pearls.

But then she did something Maggie had never seen a wealthy socialite do. She grabbed Isaac by the shoulders, brought him down to her level so he looked in her eyes and she told him, "You don't get to stop coming by just because my grandson moved across the pond." Then she wrapped her arms around him in a big hug.

Barbara sniffled and pulled away, smiling at Maggie. "This must be your new assistant." She held her hand out, not waiting for Isaac to make the introductions. "Barbara Murphy."

Still feeling more than a little shellshocked, Maggie took her hand. "Maggie Warren."

"Warren? No relation to Tobias Warren, I hope?" Barbara looked over her again, but more guarded. "There's no way you could be related. Not with that many natural curls."

Maggie hoped she kept her grimace to herself. If not, at least she kept herself from throwing an I-told-you-so look to Isaac. It was worse than she'd expected. Mrs. Murphy actually knew the Warrens. "Only related by marriage. I'm Ellis's widow."

"Oh dear, I'm sorry for your loss," Mrs Murphy said. "I was unaware he had passed."

Her honesty surprised Maggie, and though she hadn't planned to say anything else about anything having to do with the Warrens, she found herself adding, "It's been a few years."

"No matter how long it's been, it still hurts." No judgement filled Mrs. Murphy's eyes, only kindness mixed with a heap of understanding. The older woman held out her hand. "Come on inside, you'll sit next to me at lunch. I'll fill you in on widow secrets, but you must call me Barbara."

With a sense of relief, Maggie took the offered hand and walked with Barbara to the dining room.

Isaac knew he'd made the right decision to insist Maggie join him when he heard Barbara say, "I met your Ellis once, he was a good man. Nothing at all like his father."

In the short time it took to reach the dining room and to sit down, Maggie had regained her natural exuberance and it seemed possible she might actually enjoy lunch instead of merely surviving.

Barbara insisted Maggie sit next to her, and for a few minutes, he sat back and watched as they chatted. In fact, it wasn't until they were halfway through with their entrees that Barbara put her fork down and addressed him.

"Isaac," she said. "The Wall Street Fine Arts Benefit is next month. Lance had agreed to host it last year, but of course that was before a certain violin virtuoso swept him off his feet and he moved to London because that's what you do when you're in love."

He stopped himself from saying he'd never followed a woman to London. Barbara had known him since he was in middle school and would quickly remind him that of course he hadn't because he'd never been in love before.

"Normally," Barbara said. "I wouldn't mind looking elsewhere for a host, but it's only a few weeks away and I'm so far behind because Richard left and -"

"What do you mean Richard left?" Isaac asked. Richard had been Barbara's assistant for years.

Lance always joked that the man was useless, but he had to be doing something since she'd kept him around for so long.

Barbara waved her hand as if to say he was focusing on the wrong thing, but replied, "His granddaughter with the twins asked him to stay with them in Michigan for the summer."

Isaac frowned. Without Richard to help and since Lance was in London, he could easily picture Barbara running herself into the ground by agreeing to do too much. She'd done it before and wound up in the hospital. He wondered if Lance knew about Richard being in Michigan for the summer and quickly guessed he did not. "Does Lance know?" he asked.

"I can't imagine he does, I only remembered because one of the other board members asked if he'd be coming back to host."

"I meant does he know about Richard?"

"No," Barbara answered. "I'm not going to spend my time talking with Lance about Richard. He can't stand the guy."

Her grandson would like him even less if he knew he'd left her without an assistant for the summer. "With good reason from the way it sounds."

"I only need to know if you will take Lance's place and host. I don't need a running commentary."

"Of course I'll host in place of Lance." He dropped his voice, not wanting to upset her. "You know I'd do anything in my power to help you."

"Thank you," she said. "That is certainly a weight off my shoulders."

He had to treat the situation delicately. Barbara would get offended if he came on too strong, but if he didn't keep an eye on her…

He stopped that line of thinking, not even wanting to think about anything happening to the woman who'd always treated him as one of her own.

"What do you have in place for the benefit?" Maggie asked and then threw him totally off guard with her next statement. "I used to help Ellis plan events all the time. Told him once the only reason he didn't want me working full-time was so I could oversee all his events."

"Too bad Isaac's already got you working for him," Barbara said. "Or else I'd scoop you up for myself. Although…" Her eyes lit up with mischief. "I could always steal you away from him. Whatever he's paying you, I'll double."

"Oh no." Maggie shook her head. "I can't. It wouldn't be fair to Isaac, to leave him like that." She looked to him, clearly expecting him to agree with her, but Isaac wasn't so sure.

The only thought his brain could construct at the moment was that if Maggie worked for Barbara, she wouldn't be his employee anymore.

CHAPTER TWELVE

Isaac needed to change the topic of conversation, fast. "Have you talked with Celeste recently?" he asked Barbara.

"Yes." The older woman smiled. "We try to talk at least once a week. She's in Venice this week. It's one of Lance's favorite cities. He's showing her around between practices and performances."

Isaac tried not to be jealous of his oldest friend, but seriously? Touring Europe with the love of your life? Yeah, hard not to feel a little envious. "I'm glad he found someone."

"I am, too." Barbara tapped her mouth with her napkin. "I'll admit, Celeste is not the type I thought he'd settle down with, but they seem to be serious.

And I've never been more happy to be proven wrong."

Isaac turned his gaze to Maggie. "I hope you'll be able to meet them soon. You'll love Celeste."

"I look forward to it." Maggie tilted her head as if thinking about something, but whatever it was, she kept to herself.

The rest of their lunch passed uneventfully. Isaac was pleased Maggie and Barbara got along so well. Though from what he'd witnessed, Maggie got along well with everyone. So what was her in-laws problem? If he thought it'd help, he'd look them up and ask them in person. But he didn't think it'd do any good, and he was pretty certain Maggie wouldn't appreciate it.

The three of them sat in the dining room for a while even after they finished eating and everything had been cleared away. It was Barbara who called an end to the long lunch by apologizing, saying she had to leave for an afternoon appointment.

Isaac stood up, to help her out of her chair. "You don't mind if I take Maggie on a walk to see the lake, do you?"

"Not at all," Barbara insisted. "My home is your home. You two stay for as long as you like."

He waited until she left before taking Maggie

outside. She walked beside him along the well maintained walkway leading to the lake. Though Barbara had left, her house was far from empty and Isaac didn't want any ears other than his and Maggie's for the conversation he was about to initiate.

He glanced at the woman walking beside him. She'd let her hair down today and her curls bounced with every step she took. At work she wore it pulled back in a ponytail. He liked it down much better.

"What did you think of Barbara?" he asked.

"I really liked her. She's so down to earth and friendly. It's nice to know not everyone in her income bracket is a snot." She snorted, probably at something she thought, but didn't say anything else.

"She was almost like a second mother to me when Lance and I were kids. Especially after Lance's mother died and his father basically checked out." They'd made it to the lake and stood on the covered deck area often used for parties, looking out across the water. "I knew Barbara would like you as well."

"Were you aware she needed help with the party?"

"No. I didn't know about Richard either," he admitted, scratching his head. "There's no way Lance knows. I'll call him when I get home."

"Do you think she was serious about that job offer?" Maggie asked.

"Yes," he said. "She's not one to joke about something like that. What did you think of it?"

She stood unmoving. For a second he thought she might be afraid to voice her thoughts, but then he decided that didn't sound like the Maggie he knew.

"I thought," she said so low, he had to strain to hear. "I thought if I worked for her, I wouldn't be your employee."

"Do you want to be my employee?" He put a hand on her shoulder and turned her so she faced him. "Maggie?"

"It's not that I don't enjoy working for you. It's just…" She took a deep breath, but he wasn't going to help her. If she wanted it, wanted him, she could damn well say it. "It's just, if I had a choice…I'd rather be with you and play to see if I'm really kinky. I want to submit to you."

He saw her tremble. Very slight, but it was there. He held his arms out. "Come here, Maggie."

She didn't hesitate, but walked the few steps necessary to fit herself in his embrace.

"I'm so proud of you for saying that," he said into

her hair. "I know how hard it was to admit that. Even to me."

He couldn't imagine the strength it'd taken to tell her husband the same thing and then for him to treat her as if she was a freak. Then, years later, to gather the strength once again to admit, this time to her boss, what she wanted.

"I would be honored to take that journey with you," he said. "To accept your submission for however long you gift me with it. We can come back tonight or tomorrow and tell Barbara you're free to work with her."

She pulled back. "Are you sure? That would leave you without a personal assistant again."

"I've been doing some thinking," he said. "And I realized that I've worked very hard for a good number of years and perhaps it's time I stepped back and slowed down a bit."

"You?"

He smiled at the hopeful look in her eyes. "Yes. Me. And if I drop my hours, I don't think I'll need a personal assistant anymore."

"What will you do with all that time?"

He assumed she knew very well what he planned to do with that time, but he'd tell her anyway. "Before you officially hand in your resignation, we should probably make sure you know first hand what you're getting into."

"That sounds reasonable."

Reasonable left the building the day he met her, but that was beside the point. So he leaned closer and asked, "What are your plans for the rest of the day."

Only he wasn't prepared for her reply.

"Whatever you want them to be, Mr. Gregory."

His eyes flashed with shock, but only for the tiniest fraction of a second. "Is that so?" he asked.

God help her it was. "Yes, Mr. Gregory."

"In that case will you come with me to my house? I'll have you complete a checklist, we'll go over a few items, and if we both agree, maybe I'll allow you to submit to me, again. And this time there will be nothing keeping me from going as far as we want."

Although she'd been honest at the time she'd told Ty she wouldn't be ready to look at another check-list for five years, she had to admit at that second, the thought of going over one for Isaac didn't fill her with dread the way she'd imagined it would. And his mention of going as far as they wanted made her body hum. "Yes, please. Take me to your house."

She hoped he'd kiss her, but he only nodded and said, "Thank you, Maggie." He held out his hand. "Shall we?"

Oh, God, yes. She took his hand and let him lead the way back to his car.

In her life, Maggie had done many things for many people. Her parents had raised her to look for ways to help others and then to follow up with action. She never begrudged those she helped. It was the exact opposite, actually. Most of the time she wanted to do more.

But today, today was for her. This time with Isaac, for however long it lasted, was for her. She refused to feel guilty or ashamed. She would embrace it and allow herself to seek answers to the questions she'd left unanswered for so many years, she'd come close to accepting they'd always stay that way.

Isaac's hand was strong and her body yearned to feel the rest of him. She consoled herself with the knowledge she would do so soon.

HE LIVED on the top floor, in the penthouse, of

course. They didn't speak much in his private elevator, but he kept his hand on her lower back, and somehow that small touch confounded her. It was such a slight touch, almost a nothing touch, if she thought about it. Yet Isaac's hand wasn't close to slight, much less nothing. On the contrary, it was the exact opposite, almost unforgivingly possessive as it rested there, laying claim to her.

The elevator slid to a silent stop and the doors opened into his penthouse. She'd known he was wealthy based on the suit she'd ruined the day they met, but now standing in his Park Avenue penthouse, she realized she'd vastly underestimated how wealthy he was. Funny how she'd never seen him as a rich snob.

Looking around, she almost felt like asking him if he was sure he was in the right place because it didn't look as if anyone lived in the spotless apartment. But then he leaned down and whispered, "I'll be right back," and she didn't care about anything other than him.

Less than two minutes passed before he returned and led her to the living room. She sat on his couch, while he took a seat on the ottoman.

"While we're discussing the details," he said, "you may speak freely and ask any questions you have.

No need to address me as anything other than Isaac at the moment."

He held out a sheet of paper and she expected unease to hit, but all she felt was excitement. Perhaps because this time Isaac sat in front of her and they would do things on the list?

Hell to the yes.

"I know you filled one out at the club," he said. "But this one is different."

She took her time and found it was easier this time than it had been at the club. Some of that had to do with the internet research she'd done. But part of it came from imagining Isaac doing things to her or commanding her to do them to him. And some items on the list at the club weren't on his list at all.

When she finished, she handed it to him and he glanced at it before putting it aside. "I don't think we'll do anything too wild and crazy tonight," he said. "Do you have safewords you want to use or do you prefer *green*, *yellow*, and *red*?"

Safewords. Finally. After years of wishing she could play, and too many fantasies to count, she was finally going to make them a reality. "I've always planned on using *green*, *yellow*, and *red*."

"We'll use those then," he said. "Any questions about anything on the checklist?"

"No." Everything had been straightforward.

"Any burning questions before I bring up a few things?"

"Nothing that comes to mind right away."

"Tell me," he said. "Is your full name Margaret?"

She wrinkled her nose. "Yes, but I've never used it. Never seemed to suit me. I always felt more like a Maggie than a Margaret."

"Would you have an issue with me calling you Margaret during our play sessions?"

Why when he put it that way did it sound like the hottest thing ever? Damn, only Isaac had the ability to make her long for someone to call her by her full name. Not just someone, though. She knew she'd only ever want one person, one man, to call her Margaret.

Only Isaac.

"No." She shivered at the thought of hearing him say, 'Margaret' in that low, commanding, no nonsense voice of his. "I think I would like that very much."

"What are you thinking right now?"

She bit back a nervous giggle. "Remember the first day we met, and I asked about you commanding people?"

"Yes."

"I wanted you to command me, and it never occurred to me that it would ever happen and I'm so... happy. Does that sound silly?" She hoped she didn't come across as a silly woman, that was the last thing she wanted.

"No," he said. "And don't ever hold back saying what you think or how you feel. I will never think less of you for being honest. The one sure way to upset or disappoint me; however, is for you to keep things to yourself or for you to be dishonest. Do you understand?"

"Yes," she said, and then added, "Can I call you 'Sir' now?"

"Do you have anymore questions?"

"Not at the moment."

"Then, yes, you may. In fact, if you'd like to continue, stand up and strip. Once you're naked, go to the middle of the room and kneel for me."

CHAPTER THIRTEEN

MAGGIE KNEW she'd heard him correctly, but really? Right here in the living room? Even if he didn't have a playroom, wouldn't a bedroom be better? But then it hit her she would be naked and in front of Isaac. Did it matter which room they were in?

No, it didn't. Not in the least.

Moving quickly so he wouldn't think she wasn't interested, she stood and disrobed, not bothering to fold or put her clothes in a neat pile. She walked to the center of the room and wasn't sure she took a breath until she knelt.

From behind her, Isaac's footsteps sounded, but didn't seem as if they were getting closer. Was he going somewhere? She'd never appreciated how difficult it was to hold still and not look at whatever she wanted to until that exact moment.

"You need to come back over here and put your clothes somewhere neatly," he said. "That means folded and in a pile."

He was joking, right? She was naked and waiting for him. He'd just had her complete a kink checklist. There was no way he could be serious about her putting her clothes away.

Except, he didn't sound like he was joking. She slowly stood, just in case he came back with a laugh and 'just kidding.' But he didn't. He stood behind her clothes with his arms crossed, waiting.

She took her pants first and folded them.

"As you may have noticed," he said. "I don't leave things hanging around in here just any old way and I would ask that you do the same when you're here. If it bothers you I'm asking you to do something that may not appear kink-related, look on it like you are showing me respect when you treat my house with respect. Does that make sense?"

"Yes, Sir," she replied. It did when he explained it that way. So much sense she kind of hated she hadn't thought of it before he said something. Everything she'd had on was now in a pile which she placed on the end of the couch.

"Very nice, Margaret," he said when she made it back to the center of the room and knelt down.

"I'm sorry, Sir," she said.

"There's no need to apologize," he was quick to tell her. "I hadn't given you any commands or guidelines, so there's no way you could have known my preferences."

"Even so," she said. "I feel as though it's so obvious, I should have known."

"Look at it this way, you didn't know before, but now you do. And if it happens again, I will not withhold correcting you."

Sweet fuck, it shouldn't turn her on like that when he talked about the possibility of punishing her. What did it say about her that it did?

"Whenever I ask for you to wait for me somewhere, this position you're in now is how I want to find you. Understood?"

"Yes, Sir," she said, and in that minute, she realized she didn't like calling him "Sir." It sounded too generic, especially since he'd already told her submissives always called him 'Sir' during play. Now; however, was not the time to be thinking about anything other than what he was talking about.

"Very good, Margaret. Stand up and face me, please."

Her pulse raced as if she'd just consumed an entire pot of coffee herself. How was it possible he looked even more attractive when he stood there all Dom-like? He took a step closer, so close if she reached out a hand, she'd touch him. But she wouldn't because he'd told her once not to touch him when they were in a scene. And if she didn't, maybe either he'd touch her or else he'd allow her to touch him.

"I should have said this before," he said. "But just so you know, I'm not one for casual relationships. When I play with a submissive, I'm monogamous. I would ask the same from you."

"I'm not seeing anyone, Sir," she told him. "Haven't been out with anyone in a long time." What she could have added but didn't, was what man could she even fathom going out with if he was her's exclusively?

"But you're a beautiful woman," he said. "Are you sure you're okay giving up potential dates with other guys?"

"My only desire is for you, Sir." She made sure she looked him in the eyes as she spoke.

His eyes grew dark, and he made a noise low in

his throat she swore sounded like a growl. "It pleases me to hear you say that, Margaret. You have no idea what it does to me."

She forced herself not to touch him. Funny how she'd never thought that would be difficult. "I would have a better idea about what it did to you if you would show me, Sir."

A seductive grin quickly replaced his look of surprise. "You would, wouldn't you?" He took a step closer, nearly obliterating any space between them. "Put your hand out and touch my cock through my pants."

Yes. Finally.

She gasped at how large and hard he felt under her fingers.

He continued talking as she followed his command. "That's it. Touch it and see how hard thoughts of you have made it. Right now, it's begging me to take my pants off and push you face down over the arm of the sofa."

She kept her hand on him since he didn't tell her to move, but God, she wanted to shove her hand under his waistband and feel him skin-on-skin. Then she wanted to bend over the arm of his sofa and offer herself to him.

"Margaret."

She jumped at the sound of her name. "Sir?"

"You're thinking too much. I'm not sure about what, but you're too deep inside your mind."

How did he know? "Sir?" she asked again, because was he a mind-reader or something?

"It doesn't take much in the way of observational skills to see unnecessary thoughts preoccupy your mind at the moment. When you and I are together like this, I'm to be the only thing you need concern yourself with. Understand?"

She frowned. How was that possible? Could you work your brain like that? "I understand what you're saying, Sir. I'm not sure how to do it. It's like when someone tells you not to think about a duck and all you can think about are ducks."

He didn't speak, and she hoped he was thinking about ways to help her and not wishing he'd never agreed to this.

"Maybe you would find it beneficial to picture my words in your mind as I say them," he said, and it sounded reasonable to her. "That way, you're thinking, but only about what I said."

"I like the way it sounds," she said. "I'll try it, Sir."

He nodded. "Tell me what your top three fantasies were when you thought about being in a power exchange scene."

She exhaled deeply. Wow, talk about jumping straight in the deep end. However, she never thought about being anything less than truthful. "Number one is anal sex. Number two would be a capture fantasy. And number three," she thought for a minute, "probably double penetration."

"I plan on sending you home with a copy of my checklist," he said. "But just so you're aware, sharing is a hard limit of mine. I'm not opposed to double penetration as long as another man isn't involved. Is that acceptable to you?"

She bit back a laugh.

"Are you laughing at me, Margaret?"

"No, Sir," she said, unable to stop her grin.

"Obviously, something amused you."

"Yes, Sir," she replied but hastened to add, "It's not really you, but something you said, or more to the point, how you said it."

He remained silent, no doubt wanting her to continue.

"You told me to picture everything you said in my mind, right, Sir?" she asked.

"Yes," he said with a hint of hesitation.

"Everything you say, I picture as words written in Comic Sans," she said. "And double penetration looks funny in that font."

"I see," he said, and she stopped herself from asking what it was he saw. "It's going to take a bit more in order for me and only me to get inside your head. Lucky for us both, we have plenty of time. Let's start with you bent over the arm of the couch."

Needless to say, his plan was already working because she didn't picture any of those words in any font whatsoever. She hurried to get into the position he asked and once there, found only Isaac in her mind. She wasn't about to tell him his plan already worked. Not when she was finally in a position for him to do something.

"Spread your legs more," he said from somewhere behind her. "I want a good look at everything it is you're offering."

She would die if all he did was look. She would die so dead. Damn, she thought as she moved her legs the way he'd asked. What if all he did was look today?

But from behind her came his footsteps, even and steady as he walked across the hardwood floor. She held her breath as he drew nearer.

"No, Margaret," he said. "We can't have that. You need to breathe. Inhale."

She followed his command.

"Good girl. Exhale."

He repeated the exercise a few more times and she, surprisingly, felt more relaxed when he stopped.

Until his hand brushed her ass. "You're beautiful, Margaret."

She'd never felt particularly beautiful at any point in her life with the possible exception of her wedding day. That didn't count in her mind, because ninety-nine percent of women probably felt the same way. And the truth was, while she didn't have a problem with nudity, being naked never made her feel beautiful. Besides, naked people looked funny. She didn't think she'd ever looked at a naked person and thought they were beautiful.

"Lost inside your mind again, I see." His voice was a combination of amusement and resolve. "I see we're going to have to do this the hard way."

Her body tensed at what he meant by 'the hard way'. Naked didn't didn't seem so funny anymore.

But no sooner had she tensed, then both of his hands were on her, stroking down her back. "Relax, Margaret. Let go. Let your body feel. And let your-self get lost in my touch, because I'm watching over you and I'll always get you home safely. That is my solemn vow to you."

How could she do anything else when he made a promise like that? She took one more deep breath and allowed her body to sink into the sensation of him.

He responded by trailing kisses along her spine. That part of her had to be hyperaware because every brush of his lips against her skin felt magnified and she lifted her back up, wanting more of him.

"Be still," he whispered and swept his fingers down her side from her neck to her waist. "Just feel. Don't anticipate. Don't try to guess."

As they progressed further and further into the scene, she found it easier and easier to obey. The more he spoke, the more she listened. With each command he gave, she prayed another would follow. Her entire being focused on him, his voice, and his touch.

His teeth nipped the swell of her ass and she gasped because that had never been part of any fantasy and that was a damn shame. He did it again. Harder.

"Oh, yes. More," she begged.

He smacked her backside with a sharp slap, and she squealed. It was unfair for him to be so unaffected when she was melting into a puddle of girl goo. He dragged a finger from the back of her knee, up the inside of her thigh, and lightly skimmed her entrance.

"Fuck, you're soaked."

The roughness of his voice proved he was not as unaffected as she'd thought and she smiled inwardly. He slipped a finger inside her, making the smile disappear with a sharp intake of breath. For several long minutes he continued, taking his time and working first one finger and then two inside her.

"You're so tight and wet," he muttered while he kept teasing her with his fingers. "It makes me so hard thinking about slipping my cock inside you. To push myself into that wet heat and feel you wrapped around me, your body stretching as I fuck my way deeper and deeper."

"Sir. Please." She didn't want to come until he granted permission, but holy hell, the way he talked made it difficult for her to hold back.

"Oh, no," he said. "Don't even think about coming. I'm not anywhere near finished with you."

What? He had to be kidding. "Sir?"

"The least I can do today is explore one of your fantasies." He slipped his fingers out of her and circled her anus. "Don't you think?"

She couldn't think of anything at the moment. "Huh?"

"Of course, do you know what's better than exploring one fantasy?"

"No, Sir."

"Exploring two." Having said that, he moved off to the side for a second.

The next thing she felt wasn't his finger, but something wet dribbled between her ass cheeks. He was going there today? She'd thought it'd be at least a few weeks before he even brought anal sex up.

"Uh, Sir?" She didn't wait, but rushed ahead, wanting to get the words out. "I don't think...." Her voice trailed off because he suddenly appeared before her.

"Did you mean to say 'red?'" he asked.

"No, Sir."

"Did you mean to say 'yellow?'"

"No, Sir."

"In that case, I'll continue and you'll be quiet." He moved behind her again. "I only want you to speak if you're using a safeword or answering a question I asked you."

She remained silent, not only because he was right, but because she'd been aroused by the firm and uncompromising way he'd responded. Though she'd expected he'd turn her on with what he did to her, she wouldn't have guessed the same thing would happen by him correcting her. It was a fairly big revelation to her, but Isaac kept talking, so she put it aside to think about later.

"What I'll show you today isn't exactly the same as two men taking you." He chuckled. "I'm a very possessive Dom and I told you I don't like to share. But if I'm reading you right, you like that about me."

She did like that, and even though some part of her would always wonder what it would be like to have sex with two men, she was content not to actually have the experience.

He slapped her ass. Fuck. That felt good.

Something cold and hard pressed against her anus; she clenched her butt cheeks as hard as she could. His smack to her ass this time was considerably harder and didn't feel nearly as good.

"You have to relax," he said. "I have ways to make it almost impossible for you to tighten up on me, but you won't like them."

That didn't sound like anything she wanted to experience. With a shaky voice, she said, "I'm sorry, Sir. I won't clench the next time." She braced for his touch, ready for the cold and unyielding press of whatever it was he held.

But when his touch came it wasn't any of those. He ran both hands over the expanse of her back. "Margaret," he said. "Do you trust me?"

What an absurd question. Of course she trusted him. Did he think she'd be here in the position she was in if she didn't? "Yes, Sir."

"Do you think I would reward that trust by doing something that had the potential to put you off kink forever?"

Not when he put it that way, she didn't. "No, Sir," she admitted.

"Thank you for that. So with that in mind do you think you should expect to enjoy or hate what I have planned?"

It sounded so sensible when he said it. Why couldn't she make that much sense in her own mind? "Enjoy, Sir."

"Yes. Now, don't clench." His hands were back, soothing and sensual, just as before, but this time she allowed him to take her wherever he wanted. She took deep, even breaths, and focused on keeping her body relaxed. "That's my girl." His praise filled her with warmth from the inside out and she longed to sink deeper and deeper into that warmth.

One of his hands moved between her legs, stroking her where she was oh-so-empty. She wanted so badly to lift her hips up, to beg him with her body for more, to fill her, to make her come. But she found she didn't have the drive. All she wanted was to stay where she was and allow him to direct where she went.

He said something else, and though she couldn't make out the words, she understood the tone, and that alone made her warm again. His other hand drifted across her body and though she knew where it was headed, it didn't make her anxious this time. Especially with the way the hand between her legs kept bringing her closer and closer to the release she knew wasn't far away.

His fingers circled her rear opening and she took a deep breath, humming, because it actually felt good the way he was touching her. Both his hands worked in tandem, bringing her closer and closer. She heard a whimper and it shocked her to realize it was her.

"I've got you," he promised, low and deep, strong and sure. She believed him and went where he took her.

A finger pressed inside her from each of his hands and she didn't pull away. She didn't ever want it to end. He chuckled and she realized she must have spoken that out loud.

But he didn't speed up, he slowed down, and she groaned and begged to no avail.

It hit her then what she needed to say. "Green," she said, loud and strong and clear. "Green."

"Good job," he said, his voice filled with pride. Something hard and unyielding pressed against her back entrance, and she allowed it inside. She took a deep shuddering breath as the pleasure intensified between her legs.

And just as she asked, he increased his speed and his touch, and she was getting closer and closer still. His thumb stroked across her clit and she almost lost it.

"Yes, Margaret," he said. "Yes. Let yourself go. I've got you. I'll always have you."

She jumped and let him catch her.

CHAPTER FOURTEEN

ON MONDAY, Maggie walked into Isaac's office as soon as she arrived, a coffee for him in one hand and a letter for him in the other. He took the coffee with a 'thank you' and placed it on his desk.

"Is that what I think it is?" he asked, raising an eyebrow.

"I guess that all depends on what you think it is." She tried to keep her voice as nonchalant as possible and was pleased that she did a good job.

He stood up from his desk and towered over her. "Is that a letter ending your employment with me, thereby removing all the reasons I had for not pushing you over my desk and fucking you as hard as I could?"

His coarse words had her swooning and ready to

153

shove everything off his desk. Instead, she gave a low whistle. "I had no idea 'thereby' could be such a hot word, but you somehow made it sexy."

He growled but otherwise remained silent.

"And," she continued, "I hope it's okay but my new employer needs me to start as soon as possible, so I can't work a notice. Today is my last day."

He'd been on the first part of her call with Barbara, so none of this came as a surprise to him. In fact, he was the one who told her a notice wasn't necessary. But acting it out in his office was fuck hot. Almost like a role play.

"If that's the case, you can leave now. There's no reason for you to stay." He motioned with his head toward the door. "You know the way out."

Those were his words, but his body didn't agree based on his erection and the mischief in his eyes told a different story as well. He didn't want her to leave yet.

"If I may, Sir." She ran her hand up his chest. "There's one thing I'd like to know for certain before I leave."

"What would that be?"

She cupped him through his pants. "I've heard rumors about you. Specifically about a certain part of your anatomy, and I really need to know if these rumors are true."

"You do, do you?"

"Yes, Sir."

He put his hand over hers. Stopping her from moving it further. "There's a price you have to pay to see my cock in this office."

Her heart raced and wetness pooled in her panties. "What price is that?"

"Suck it for as long as it takes for me to get off."

Yes. She tilted her head as if thinking. "How long will that take?"

He shrugged. "Could be five minutes. Could be five hours. Who knows?"

She bit her bottom lip not missing how his eyes fixated on her mouth. Wanting to tease him, she stuck the tip of her tongue out and licked the spot where her teeth had just been. He moaned low in his throat.

"Deal," she said, and bent her knees so she could kneel before him.

"No, not there," he said, putting a hand out to stop her. "Go get under my desk. I have a lot of work to do since you resigned."

It was wicked and she loved it. Making her way

under the desk, she couldn't help but think of the time she tried to give Ellis a blow job while he was driving. He'd been flabbergasted and told her to stop it immediately. She didn't listen and he wound up pulling over and off the road. He allowed her to finish, but then he read her the riot act, telling her she'd done a damn dangerous thing that could have gotten them killed.

That was the last time she'd initiated anything sexual. He'd died a few weeks later.

Sitting in her current position under Isaac's desk, she was only able to see his chair. But on the positive side, no one could see her unless they walked around his desk.

Ellis would have flipped his shit at the mere thought of her blowing him in his office. She frowned. Why did Ellis keep popping into her mind today?

A knock on Isaac's office door kept her from thinking further about her late husband.

She heard the door open.

"Nina," Isaac said. "What can I help you with?"

"I'm looking for Maggie. Is she in here? Have you seen her?" the admin asked.

"I saw her when she first came in," Isaac answered. "Is she not at her desk?"

"No, I went by there first." Nina sighed. "If you see her, tell her I'm looking for her."

"I'll be sure to do that," Isaac said, and the door clicked shut.

His footsteps sounded as he made his way to his desk. He pulled out his chair and sat down without looking at her once.

"Nina's looking for you." He unzipped his pants and took his cock out. "Get busy." Without waiting to ensure she'd do as he asked, he picked up his office phone, clearly ready to get back to work.

What did it say about her that she became so aroused when he treated her like little more than a sex toy? Why was she having to force herself not to slip her hand between her legs for just a little relief? But more than that, why did she feel better than she had in years, scrunched up under an office desk, eyeing what had to be the biggest dick she'd ever seen?

Granted, she was no cock connoisseur, but she'd seen her share.

"Excuse me," Isaac said from above her and the phone clicked as he muted the link. "Is there a reason why your mouth isn't full of dick, Margaret?"

"Just admiring the view, Sir."

"Admire it with the back of your throat."

She knew better than to make him wait. Before he had the phone unmuted, her lips were around the head of his cock and she was in the process of taking him in as far as she could.

"Sorry about that," he said to whoever he'd called. "Now…"

She blocked out the boring ass work call he was on and focused her attention on his dick. It wouldn't help anything to think about how long it'd been since she'd given anyone a blow job. Or that she'd never tried to deep throat before. She took her time, taking him as deep as she could, pulling back to grab some air, and then taking him again. Each time she found she was able to take a little bit more than the time before.

Determined, she focused only on the task at hand. Each centimeter she considered a victory and after every victory, she gave herself a mental high-five. She also decided she'd never view the term cocksucker as a negative again. Every other person in the world be damned.

"Fuck, that's so good," Isaac said and her concentration faltered for a minute.

When had his phone call ended? She wasn't surprised she hadn't heard him telling the other person goodbye or been aware of him hanging up.

What surprised her was she didn't remember him touching her hair, but she was certain one of his hands rested on her curls

"Hold still," he said, fisting her hair and removing any lingering doubt about his hand. With powerful thrusts he fucked her mouth, all the while ensuring he never went deeper than she could manage.

"I'm going to come and you're going to swallow."

For a minute she was disappointed. She'd wanted him to come on her and mark her as his. But on second thought, his way was more practical. They were in his office, and she had a meeting in the afternoon with Barbara. What would be sexy now, would lead to uncomfortable moments, not only on her part but on the people she'd interact with later as well. They could always do that version of sexy later.

A few more thrusts and he exploded into her mouth. She managed not to spill one drop. He fixed his pants and then pulled her up to sit on his lap for a minute. His arms were heaven and for several long moments, she simply enjoyed the feel of them around her.

"You are amazing, Maggie." He kissed her forehead. "It's probably for the best that today's your last day. If it wasn't, you might have found yourself chained underneath my desk for the foreseeable future."

"The way you say it makes it sound as if I wouldn't have enjoyed it."

His eyes burned her with rekindled desire. "You better go find Nina and she what she wants before I'm tempted to call Barbara and tell her I'm keeping you here and fuck what anyone thinks."

CHAPTER FIFTEEN

As MUCH AS she'd enjoyed working for Isaac, by the end of her first week with Barbara, Maggie knew the position with the older lady was a much better fit. While she'd remembered enjoying event planning with Ellis, she'd somehow forgotten how good she was at it.

More than anything, though, she adored Barbara. Her new employer considered it her new mission to challenge every assumption Maggie held about those in the upper class, but that wasn't why. The main reason was she found Barbara to be a delightful person.

It had taken only a few hours of working together for the two of them to see they made a great team. Barbara was full of ideas and visions while Maggie excelled at taking that vision and putting together a plan to bring it to life. At the end of the first day, Barbara hugged her and said she didn't care if Richard ever came back. In fact, on her way out the door not long after, Maggie overheard Barbara telling the housekeeper she might send Richard a text and tell him to stay in Michigan.

Unfortunately, because Maggie worked so many hours her first week in an effort to bring Barbara to a place where she no longer felt behind, there was no time to see Isaac. They talked every day and sent numerous texts, but they weren't able to find a time to get together. Isaac joked that if her second week was anything like her first, he'd stage an invasion and bring her back.

But now it was finally Friday night, and she waited in the lobby of his building for his private elevator. Earlier in the day he'd told her to be at his place at seven-thirty, she had surprised herself by making it to his lobby by seven-twenty. She couldn't remember the last time she'd been so early for anything.

She stepped into the elevator and in no time at all she found herself in Isaac's penthouse with the man himself standing off to the side.

"Hello, Maggie," he said. "Did you have a good day?"

"Yes, I did actually. I love Barbara," she replied effortlessly.

"I'm glad to hear the position with her is working out."

"Thank you." She couldn't help but wonder if he was glad to get rid of the mess all over her desk.

"Even though the office isn't near as lively as it was when you there," he continued and the sincerity of his words made her smile. "Why don't we sit down and chat for a bit?"

She agreed, and he led her through a set of double doors. On the other side was an outdoor area unlike anything she'd ever seen. She wasn't sure what to call it. The three exposed sides were covered with a crawling plant of some sort and sculpted flower beds lined two sides. The only way you'd know you were outside was the sky overhead.

"This is gorgeous." She walked all the way inside and turned, trying to take it all in.

Isaac followed, watching her. "It's my favorite spot to sit and think." He motioned to a comfortable looking seating area with loveseats and a small table.

He didn't speak again until she sat down and he'd

joined her. "It hit me this week we should have a schedule of sorts."

"What kind of schedule?"

"Of when we'll explore kink together." He hesitated before saying, "I don't want to make an assumption that because you want to learn about BDSM with me that you want anything else."

She looked at him sideways because his words didn't make any sense at all. "What do you mean?"

"You're a widow and even though we've discussed a few BDSM scenes, I have no idea what you want in your private and personal relationships."

She couldn't hold back her laugh even as he lifted an eyebrow at her. "I'm sorry," she said. "But hearing you say that I realized I have an idea about what I want." She wiped her eyes. "For a long time after Ellis died, I swore I'd never get married again. I mean I loved Ellis, but he ended up not being the man I thought he was, and I can't go through anything like that again."

He nodded. "I understand."

"But lately," she said, and his head shot up. The surprise in his eyes bordered on comical. "I'm not so sure. I think if the right man came along, I can see myself changing my mind."

"You can?"

"Yes, because I'd do it different the next time."

"How?"

"For one, I wouldn't hide parts of me. He'd have to love every part of me and accept every part. Not try to change them."

"That should be a given in any long term relationship," he said.

"Should be, but that doesn't mean it is."

"True. And since you've been so honest with me, I can be no less to you." He brushed an escaped curl out of her eyes and tucked it behind her ear. "I like you, Maggie, and I'd like to get to know you outside of anything kinky we explore."

"You want to date me?" Why was it so hard for her to believe he meant that?

"Yes, exactly that." He grinned for the first time since she'd arrived. "If you'll have me?"

She turned, so she faced him. "Yes," she whispered, still not sure she wasn't dreaming the entire conversation.

Isaac stood. "I've decided to change my plans. I brought you out here to go over my suggestions for your BDSM education, and we'll still have that talk. For right now, though." He held out his hand, "I see the doubt in your eyes and I can't let you go one more minute thinking I didn't mean every word."

She slipped her hand in his and stood. "What's your new plan?"

He placed a soft kiss on her forehead. "To prove how true they are and erase your doubts."

Isaac led her back inside his home, and as they walked down the hall, headed toward his bedroom, he couldn't stop thinking about the situation he currently found himself in. He'd always made it a point to avoid virgins. Not that he had anything against them, he just had no desire to be with one. For one reason, he liked his sex on the unconventional side, and two... Well, there was that nickname...

Yet for all his opinions on virgins, not once had he ever given a second thought to widows. If he'd ever thought about one, which he wasn't sure he had until he met Maggie, he felt certain he wouldn't have given a second thought about being with one.

However, now that he had met Maggie, he could admit he'd have been wrong. Interestingly enough though, not for the reasons he'd have thought. The two of them fit together nicely, if anything or anyone came between them it was Ellis.

He was an ass for even having that thought and he knew it.

He didn't begrudge Maggie's memories of her late husband. From what he could tell, the man had loved and looked after her. No, his issue with Ellis stemmed from the fact that he'd made her feel like she was messed up and wrong because of what she wanted from sex. And as a result, she carried that burden with her even years after Ellis's death.

Isaac would help her get through it because it was a burden she shouldn't have and because she was worth it. No, his main problem with Ellis was that he was dead and Isaac couldn't kick his ass.

"Look at that view!"

Maggie slipped her hand out of his and crossed his bedroom to look out his window. Isaac stood back, watching. She was such a delight to watch, the way she found joy in everything. Compared to most people he knew, she was a welcome breeze.

She looked up and met his gaze through the window's reflection. Fuck, he wanted her so badly.

"I'm guessing you didn't bring me to this room in order to show me the view?" she asked.

"No," he replied. "But it is a fabulous view. Take

your time. We're not on anyone's timetable except our own."

But she didn't turn back to the window. She walked to where he stood. "If your plan wasn't to show off your windows with the to-die-for view, what was it?"

Fuck talking. They talked enough for one day.

"I could tell you," he said, tracing the collar of her shirt with his finger. "Or I could show you."

"Option two, please." She licked her lips. "Showing is definitely a plan I can get behind. I'll show you mine and you show me yours?"

"No."

"No?"

"No," he repeated. "You aren't going to do anything except receive the pleasure I give you."

"That doesn't sound like a fun time for you."

"Trust me. It will be."

"Okay but-"

He held a finger up to her lips. "Hush. No more talking or else I'll gag you."

Her body shivered in repose to his words, but she remained silent.

"Very nice, Margaret," he said. "Now, without saying a word, undress, and get on top of my bed. On your back."

She moved quickly, and he didn't fail to notice that once she'd removed her clothes, she folded and stacked them in a neat pile she placed on the corner of his dresser. Without looking his way to see if he noticed, she scrambled to get on the bed.

Keeping his clothes on, he joined her. "You did that so well, I'm going to let you come whenever you want to tonight."

"Thank you, Sir."

He nodded, getting to work by taking her legs and spreading them. "I'm going to spend part of tonight exploring your body. Discovering all of your erogenous zones and committing them to memory. When I've found them all, I'll have you get on your hands and knees so I can ride you good and hard in a fuck you won't ever forget." He nipped the inside of her knee. "Game?"

"Please, Sir."

He traced her kneecap with his tongue. "I love hearing you say please." Moving to the other leg, he did the same thing to it. "It's a habit of mine, to make sure I treat both sides the same," he explained trailing his mouth up her body, on alert for a reaction from her, and thrilled that there were so many. Her belly button. The inside of her elbow. The hollow of her neck. The curve of her ear. And her breasts. Fuck, they were perfect.

He covered her body just like he promised, kissing, teasing, and licking. She kept her eyes closed the entire time, only opening them when he pulled away. She didn't speak, but gave him a quizzical look.

Her eyes grew wider as he got down from the bed and undressed. He stood where she could watch, slowing down when he stood before her wearing only his boxers. Acting like he wasn't so hard it was painful, he stroked his length through the material. Maggie's eyes never left his crotch.

He walked to his nightstand and took a condom from inside. Holding the package between his teeth, he pushed down on his boxers, and let his erection free. Just see what she'd do, he gave it a few hard pulls. She whimpered.

"I want you to move to your hands and knees," he said, rolling the condom on his length. "I'm harder than I think I've ever been, and it's time I made good on my promise for a long hard ride. Think you're up to it?"

She flipped around quicker than he'd expected and looked over her shoulder. "I'm up for anything you can give me, as long as it involves that cock."

Damn, he loved how playful she was. He climbed on top of the bed and pushed her head down. "Then tonight's your lucky night."

She surprised him by remaining still, even though he took his time entering her. He'd known she'd feel like heaven on his cock, but knowing it in no way came close to experiencing it. Only as he thrust himself fully inside her did he hear anything from her. Even then it was a tiny yelp.

"Does it feel good to have me deep inside you?" he asked, holding still.

She mumbled something into the bedding, but pushed her ass back so he took that as a positive.

"Hold still, then, because I'm about to make you feel even better." He moved inside her with long, deep strokes. It only took a few before her hands fisted the sheets and she tightened around him. "Going to come that quick?"

He reached between them and stroked her clit once, setting off her climax. He held still until it passed. "I fucking love that you came so quickly. You have no idea. Let's see if I can make you come again."

Taking hold of her hips with both hands, he moved faster, rocking into her harder and harder. She pushed back again, meeting him, thrust for thrust. His movements became slower and more precise. He pounded her in time with the thumping noise in his head, trying to go deeper and deeper.

He wasn't going to be able to hold out much longer. Wanting to make sure she came again, he moved one hand to her lower back and circled her clit with the other. He clenched his teeth, desperate not to come until she did.

The noise in his head pounded faster and faster, keeping up with him as he drove them both to the edge. Maggie's body tensed under him, and knowing she was close, he rocked into her once more, brushing her clit, and sending them both over.

After, the silence was deafening. He pulled Maggie close, holding her in his arms. If there was anything better than holding a satisfied woman, he didn't know what it was.

Maggie rolled over to look at him. "Pretty good thing you're the only one living on this floor with all that noise the bed was making."

"What?"

"The way the bed kept hitting the wall. I'm surprised it didn't make a hole or something."

Damn, that noise had been him? "I might have gotten a bit enthusiastic." A bit? Hell, he'd never moved the bed before. He ran his hand down her back. "I didn't hurt you, did I?"

She pushed herself up on an elbow, looking as if it was the most absurd question she'd ever been asked. "I'd have used my safeword if you'd have hurt me that way. I mean, I won't be able walk tomorrow, but it's all good."

He laughed and pulled her down for a quick kiss. "Wait until I fuck your ass, Margaret."

"I knew there was something I wanted to ask you, but I kept forgetting!"

"What was that?"

"How come there are all sorts of nicknames and stuff for submissives, but only a handful for Dominants?"

"You want a nickname for me?" It took a few seconds for him to formulate the question. He'd been certain she was going to ask about anal sex.

"Yes, the more I think about it, the more I think it's unfair and we should fix it. I want a little something I can call you when we're out and no one other than us will know the meaning. The only thing is, it can't be cute or common like *Babe* or *Honey*."

"What are you thinking?" he asked, though he wasn't sure he wanted to know.

"I keep thinking about that feeling I got in my belly when I got your text to be here at seven-thirty.

It's unconventional, but I think it works." She sat up. "What do you think of Seven-Thirty?"

"You want to call me Seven-Thirty in public?"

"Yes."

He let it roll around in his head and answered with a grin. "I like it, actually."

CHAPTER SIXTEEN

SHE HADN'T BEEN PREPARED, but Isaac convinced Maggie to spend the night. Though she told him later it really didn't take much on his part to get her to stay. Either way, he was glad she did. Sometime around midnight, after he'd turned them both to their sides, her back to his front, and he'd taken her again, but slower than before, they'd lounged in each other's arms.

She gave him details about her week with Barbara, adding again how much she liked her new employer. He asked about her work and she filled him in on the details about the upcoming Wall Street benefit. Her excitement spilled into not only her voice, but her body movements as she explained how she'd had to book someone for decorations and music. Barbara, it seemed, had somehow managed to score the hottest chef in the city at the moment to cater the event.

It wasn't until Saturday afternoon that Isaac brought up the plan he'd detailed to introduce Maggie to BDSM.

He handed her a piece of paper with the items he'd picked. "You'll notice I only have the title of scene listed, not date. You should also be aware they aren't in any particular order."

Her eyes grew big as she looked over the list.

"Any questions?" He asked.

"No, Sir. Not at the moment."

She went back to reading the paper which was fine with him because that gave him more time to watch her. He'd tossed around the idea of getting her collar. Not one like he'd offer a submissive he was in a long term relationship with, but rather a training one. He'd never collared a submissive, however, and after what amounted to hours of thinking, decided not to get a collar for Maggie. Maybe it was silly reasoning, but he didn't want his first time collaring someone to be with a training collar.

But when he drove her home later that afternoon, he couldn't escape the feeling he'd made the wrong decision.

.   .   .

WEDNESDAY NIGHT, Isaac drove to Barbara's house so he could pick Maggie up for dinner. Or at least what she thought would be dinner. Little did she know that it would be the first of many scenes he'd listed out for her on Saturday.

Based on what he knew about Ellis from hearing Maggie talk about him, he wasn't surprised her checklist revealed she'd never had sex in public. That was a damn shame and one he would take care of tonight.

He pulled into the driveway and had just put the car in park when the front door opened and Maggie came bounding down the stairs. She'd left her hair down today, or more than likely, it all escaped the hair tie she used to pull it into a ponytail. Whatever the reason, he loved watching it bounce as she made her way to his car.

"Hi! Hi! Hi!" she called coming to stop at the passenger's side.

He smiled because she'd stopped and allowed him to open the car door for her. He'd told her over the weekend it was something he wanted to do when they went out together. For some reason, he'd thought she hadn't been listening, and he was delighted to see he'd been wrong.

He gave her a quick kiss before opening her door.

"Hi yourself. Good day?"

"Average day, I'd say," she told him after he got back behind the wheel. "On the other hand, I'm extraordinarily happy about going out with you tonight."

"You are?"

"Yes," she said. "How does it feel knowing you can make me all giddy inside?"

"Did you know *you* made *me* all giddy inside?"

"I do?"

"Yes." He glanced to his side just long enough to confirm the even bigger smile she now wore. "It probably feels like that."

His day had been rather drab but then again they all felt like that since she no longer worked in the building. Funny how being in her presence for a few minutes turned drab into anything but.

He hadn't told her anything about what they were doing tonight and he knew her well enough to know it was killing her that she had no idea. He had to hand it to her, she hadn't once asked for even the slightest hint.

"It's still early," he said, deciding to reward her patience. "But I made reservations at a favorite restaurant of mine in the city."

"That sounds great," she said. "I'm famished.

Barbara and I ate lunch before noon because she had a meeting with her bridge club girls this afternoon. I got caught up working, and just now realized how hungry I am."

It seemed like he couldn't stop smiling whenever he was around Maggie. Somehow, just being in her presence made everything seem brighter. And he wasn't the only one, he'd witnessed several occasions, both with people she knew as well as strangers, that she had the same effect on.

He pulled up to the valet station at the restaurant in what felt like no time. Before he opened the door, he turned to her. "When we step out of this car you become Margret, understand?"

"And you become Seven-Thirty?"

He snorted. "Yes. I become Seven-Thirty."

The unlikelihood of his current situation nearly had him shaking his head as he took her hand and they walked to the the maitre d'. Hell, he didn't even mind her nickname for him. In fact, he was rather fond of it.

In spite of the fact it was still considered early for dinner, the restaurant was a local favorite and crowds were heavy no matter the day or time.

"Have you been here before?" he asked her once

they'd been seated in a corner table he'd requested when he made the reservation.

"No," she replied. "I've always wanted to but could never get reservations."

"In that case, I hope everything lives up to your expectations."

She blushed, obviously catching the double meaning of his words. He didn't say anything else, leaving her to ponder any unspoken clues she might have picked up on concerning his plans for the evening.

The server came by and took their order. Maggie's cheeks still held a bit of color and he found it difficult to look at anything other than her. With her hair freed from the confines of her ponytail, the humidity of the weather made her curls appear wilder than normal. However, what truly captivated those around her were her eyes. The low light of the restaurant paired with the romantic glow of the candles made the green sparkle more than usual.

With their order placed and beverage glasses topped off, there was no reason for anyone to come by their table anytime soon.

"As you may have guessed," he said. "We're going to play in public tonight."

"We are, Sir?" She looked around the room. "Isn't

that a bit advanced for me?"

"No, it's not because it's not too advanced for me, and as long as you follow my directions and do exactly what I ask the way I ask, no one will be able to tell we're doing anything other than eating dinner."

She bit the corner of her mouth. If he had to guess, she was struggling between trusting him and his assertion he had everything under control and her own mind that was no doubt sending a message she was crazy for even considering such a thing.

He had to get her out of her mind.

He leaned forward. "Slip your hand up your dress, push your panties to the side, and tell me if you're wet."

She gasped, looking around as if to determine if anyone heard. They hadn't. He knew what he was doing, and he was confident in his ability to keep what they were doing hidden from anyone else. He needed to get her to that point.

"Now, Margaret," he said. "Why do you think I picked a restaurant with such long tablecloths?"

He saw the change in her expression the second she made up her mind, the slow change from turmoil to peace. Desire and excitement replaced her fear. He was so proud, he wanted to shout, but doing so wouldn't ensure they remained hidden.

One of Maggie's hands drifted below the table.

"Good girl," he whispered. "Tell me how wet you are."

Her eyelids fluttered and a quiet moan escaped her lips. "I'm so wet, Sir."

"Show me. Without looking at anything other than me." One way or another, he planned on taking up residence in her mind.

Keeping her eyes locked on his, she lifted her hand up. The evidence of how turned on she was glistened in the low light.

"Someone finds the idea of public play arousing despite her protests." He lowered his voice even more. "Now I want you to take your panties off."

"Here, Sir?" she asked, but kept her gaze on him.

"I don't recall telling you to go somewhere else." He held out his hand. "Take them off."

She didn't hesitate, dropping both hands down to her lap this time. Out of the corner of his eye, he noted a man about their age who appeared to be walking toward them. But that couldn't be, could it?

So why was the man getting closer?

"I can't believe it," the strange man said as he

approached their table. "Maggie Warren, it is you! I haven't seen you in years. How have you been?"

Maggie was as surprised, if not more, than the man now standing by their table. Her cheeks flushed a deep red, but Isaac wasn't sure if that was a result of having her hands up her skirt or because she hadn't thought to ever run into the guy standing next to her again.

Isaac stood to defuse any potential embarrassment on Maggie's behalf. "Isaac Gregory," he said, holding out his hand toward the intruder.

"Philip Conrad," the man said, shaking his hand. "Nice to meet you." And that was all the interest Philip had in Isaac. He turned back to Maggie. "Are you still living in the city?"

Maggie, who still had her hands in her lap, looked to Isaac. All too late, he realized she was probably asking for permission to speak. He wanted to say she couldn't, but that would be rude and more than likely would tip Philip off that there was more going on than dinner at their table. Reluctantly, he nodded.

"Yes," Maggie said. "I'm still here. Working for Barbara Murphy."

Philip nodded. "I know who she is. Met her once

at some charity thing for a scholarship. Music, I think."

"That's Barbara," Maggie confirmed.

Philip tilted his head and narrowed his eyes. "I always wondered why you never returned my calls after that night we went out. There were rumors you were keeping to yourself and not going out anymore. I knew they couldn't be right. Not my Maggie. It's good to see I was right."

"Actually…" Maggie said, but Philip didn't seem to hear.

"Give me a call if you want to get together sometime," Philip said. "Nice to meet you, Ian."

Isaac collected his thoughts as Philip walked away. It wasn't a big deal they had ran into an old flame of Maggie's. The fact she had an old flame wasn't a big deal either. She'd never said there had been no men in her life since Ellis died; that had been an assumption on his part. Obviously, he had been wrong.

But across the table, the color had drained from her face.

"Maggie, is everything okay?" he asked.

She shook her head. "I'm sorry."

"I don't know of anything you should apologize for."

"About six months after Ellis died, I went a little wild," she said. "Nothing heavy like drugs or anything. But drinking and dancing, yes. I dated around, too. It's embarrassing to think about now. I felt free and then I felt guilty and I learned if I partied enough, the guilt became easier to ignore. At least for a while."

"I think that sounds completely normal." It hurt him to see her this way. She was always filled with so much joy, so much life, to see her filled with anything else made him want to pull her close and protect her from the world.

"Word eventually made it to his parents, especially his mom," she continued. "Until then, they had been distant and cool, but after that, they didn't hold back how much they hated me or at least she didn't. That's when she started saying I'd killed him."

At that moment he realized it wasn't enough to protect her from the world, he needed to slay a few dragons as well.

CHAPTER SEVENTEEN

MAGGIE WASN'T sure what she'd done to have a man like Isaac in her life, but she wasn't going to complain. He was simply amazing. Even beyond the sex god part. She'd never experienced unconditional acceptance from anyone before and at times, she still didn't know what to make of it.

After that horrid moment when Philip walked up to the table, right as she'd been seconds away from handing Isaac her panties, she'd known Isaac would want nothing more to do with her. She'd never been so glad to be so wrong.

Isaac had sensed her need to get away from there, and instead of making a big production or complain about how she'd ruined dinner, he'd called the server over and asked for their food to be packed to go. He drove them to his place, where he put everything in the refrigerator, took her hand, and led her to the massive tub in his bathroom. He drew her a bath and stayed by the tub while she soaked and relaxed.

She'd asked him to join her, but he declined saying it'd be too hard for her to relax with a cock pressed against her back. Even when she rolled her eyes and told him it wasn't like the run-in with Philip had been that bad, he only replied with, "Let me take care of you, Maggie."

That was when she admitted to herself she'd fallen in love with him.

She wasn't sure what to do with that revelation, so she did nothing, keeping it wrapped up and hidden away from everyone.

TONIGHT WAS A TUESDAY, and she'd left Barbara's early because her bridge ladies were coming over for an impromptu card game/meeting. Barbara had invited her to stay, but she had a plan to surprise Isaac she'd been working on and this was the perfect day to set it up.

He'd given her a card to his elevator and informed the lobby staff she was free to come and go as she pleased.

She told the doorman to have a nice afternoon and had to hold herself back from skipping to the elevator. A quick scan of his penthouse confirmed he hadn't arrived yet.

Working quickly, she took off all her clothes, leaving them folded and in a neat pile beside the elevator. With that taken care of, she looked around for the perfect spot, knelt and waited.

It couldn't have been ten minutes before she heard the elevator descend to the lobby. She took a deep breath and didn't exhale until she heard the doors open, signaling his arrival.

She knew when he saw her from his sharp intake of breath. "If this isn't the best welcome home I've ever received, I don't know what is."

"Thank you, Sir."

"Any particular reason?" he asked. "Or just because?"

"Just because, Sir." *Just because I love you and don't know how to tell you. Just because I want to thank you for being so perfect but all the words sound cheesy and inadequate.*

Just because.

"Is that your cell phone?" he asked right as she noticed the special ring tone she'd added days ago.

"Yes, and it's Barbara. Probably a butt dial. Her bridge ladies are over."

She thought that would be the end of it, but no sooner had "Hail to the Queen" stopped than it started again. Worried, she stood. One call she could pass off as a butt dial, but two? Not likely.

Of course, by the time she reached her phone, it had stopped. Would Barbara leave a message or try calling again? No immediate call came through, and she'd just pulled up her contact list when Isaac's phone rang. He took it out of his pocket.

"Is it...." was all she managed to get out, but he understood and nodded.

"Barbara," he said, answering and Maggie hated she could only hear half of the conversation. "Yes, she's here just not able to make it to the phone in time. What's going on?"

He winced at her reply. "Barbara….. Barbara…. Listen to me. Take a deep breath, calm down, and tell me what's going on."

More silence as she answered. Isaac didn't wince again, in fact, his expression was unreadable. His words, however, told a different story.

"He called you today?"

"Isn't that a breach of contract?"

A sigh and then, "Barbara, you know better."

"Go rest and don't think about this until tomorrow…. Yes, you can…. Don't make me call Lance."

"We'll take care of it. Go rest."

He ended the call and ran his fingers through his hair. "The chef called today and said he wasn't doing the benefit. Said it was a conflict of interest or something. She's not sure exactly because she was too upset to pay attention. And to top it off, they never signed a contract. I wish you'd been working for her then, you'd have made sure that prick chef signed a contract."

Maggie's heart sank, not only because of Barbara's excitement at booking the chef in question, but also because it was going to be next to impossible to find a replacement. She started to sit down and remembered she was naked. "I'll go put my clothes on and make calls, but the benefit is next weekend. I can't imagine there's anyone with availability, and if there is, I don't see them being someone we'd want."

"Agreed," he said. "I guess the best we can hope for is that some bride or groom getting married next weekend has a horrible case of cold feet and calls off their wedding, freeing up a caterer in the process."

She felt bad wishing such a travesty on someone, but after three hours and too many dead end phone calls to count, a last minute cancellation appeared to be their only hope.

"Seriously," she told Isaac as he walked back into the living room after making calls of his own. "Even the bad caterers are booked."

He sat beside her, the slight nod of his head the only indication he'd heard what she'd said. She raised an eyebrow at his silence. As normal, she couldn't read his expression, but there was an energy pulsing through him. The more she looked at him, the more pissed he seemed to become.

"What happened?" she asked, not bothering to ask if anything had happened. That much was obvious.

"What do you know about the Warren's interest in the food industry?" he asked.

What did that have to do with anything related to their current predicament?

"I didn't know they had one."

"That's what I thought," he said. He took a deep breath. "The Warrens have recently purchased a controlling interest in that chef's restaurant. The one Barbara booked for the benefit. The contract prohibits him from working for any charity foundation not endorsed by the Warrens."

"That's the most absurd thing I've ever heard of. Who gets their panties in a wad over charities?" She had to think this through. "Why would they even care which charity he worked for? A job is a job, and you'd think they'd be happy he was bringing in money."

"You would think," Isaac agreed.

An unwelcome thought entered her mind. It turned her stomach to think it, much less voice it, but she had no choice. "Do you think this has something to do with me?"

"Do you?" he asked, and his even tone led her to believe he'd realized the possibility before she did.

"Part of me says no because you'd have to be really sick in the head to do something like that." She closed her eyes. "But the truth is, I can see them being that petty."

He reached out, and she willingly went into his arms. "I'm sorry," he said. "Sorry you have to deal with such assholes."

Oddly enough, though the Warren's actions angered her, that wasn't her prevailing emotion. Mostly she felt determined. "It's okay," she said. "I'm going to make this the best benefit you Wall Street types have ever seen."

"That's my girl," he whispered into her hair.

If she only had a clue about how to make that happen.

SHE DIDN'T SLEEP much that night. It was impossible with her mind running through ideas at eighty miles an hour. But she was thankful, otherwise she'd be thinking about the Warrens, and they didn't deserve her thoughts. By the time dawn peeked into the bedroom, she had a plan. Granted, in her current state of mind, she wasn't sure if it was the most brilliant plan ever or flaming horse shit on a stick. She drifted off to sleep, deciding she'd figure it out in a few hours.

IT TOOK three cups of coffee before her mind felt clear enough to discuss her idea with Isaac. She wanted his opinion before she took it to Barbara. She found him in the outside room, frowning at his laptop.

"You shouldn't make that frowny face," she teased, walking over to him. "You'll get wrinkly and old looking."

He closed his laptop. "Then come over here and give me something to smile about."

She sat down beside him on the loveseat. "I have an idea for the benefit and I want to run it by you before I mention it to Barbara."

"I'm all ears."

"A favorite author of mine had a new release last week. A historical romance. In it the characters attend a basket social. What happens is the women of the town each make a basket lunch. Then the men of the town bid on the basket they want and the winner gets to share his basket with the woman who made it."

"I think I read about those once," Isaac said.

"I was thinking we could do something similar. Most of the people coming are couples, but there are some singles. We ask each couple to bring a basket for two and each single a basket for one. That way everyone's paired up for dinner. But the best part is we save money by not having to pay for food or servers, and all the basket money goes to the charities the benefit is for. The biggest obstacles are making sure everyone attending is notified, like yesterday, and ensuring there's a system put in place at the venue to organize and make the basket process run as smoothly as possible."

Finished, she sat back in her seat, waiting for Isaac to say something. Her heart sank when he stood up and paced. She'd never seen him do that before. He obviously thought it was a bad idea and was thinking of a way to tell her. She watched him make two more passes across the floor and was getting ready to tell him to just forget about it when he stopped in front of her, eyes dancing.

She held her breath.

"It's brilliant," he said, and she exhaled in a big whoosh.

"It is?" she asked, wanting to make sure she heard him correctly.

"Yes," he confirmed. Not only is it brilliant, but I've never seen it done before. And we can put a positive spin on it from the start. Something like, "In an effort to streamline cost while ensuring as much of the collected funds go to those who truly need them, the Board has decided yada, yada, yada." His face broke into a huge smile. "Not just brilliant. It's fucking genius."

CHAPTER EIGHTEEN

INSTEAD OF CALLING Barbara to tell her about the idea, Maggie wanted to tell her in person. Isaac drove her to the Murphy house and witnessed Barbara's reaction.

"It's so crazy, it'll be the talk of Wall Street and the Arts world for weeks," the older woman said. "Making all the snooty arts patrons bring their own food to a party and then pay to eat what someone else brought? It's perfect! It'll be so much fun watching everyone try to one up everyone else with their baskets."

Maggie beamed from where she stood in the living room. She'd told Barbara earlier she was too excited to sit down. "We need to let all the attendees know, right away. And work out some of the logistics with food allergies, vegans, and what have you."

Barbara walked toward the hallway. "I'll go to my office and get the final guest list, we'll divide it into thirds, and the three of us will call everyone. Shouldn't be over fifteen or so calls each if we do it that way."

"We'll need to send a follow-up email after the call," Maggie said. "I'll draft it while you get the guest list."

"It may be awhile," Barbara said. "I'm also going to email Robert and tell him to stay in Michigan and enjoy more time with his family because I no longer require his assistance."

"Did she just say what I think she did?" Maggie asked him as Barbara's footsteps echoed down the hall.

"She did." And he couldn't be happier. "Looks like you're stuck here with us snooty, rich people for the foreseeable future."

"That's okay. You guys are starting to grow on me." She sighed. "I guess I can put up with you for a little longer."

He loved her playful spirit, her optimistic outlook, and nurturing nature. Nothing would make him happier than for her to stay where she was for longer. Or forever. The truth hit him and he froze. *He loved her.*

He'd never expected to fall in love, mostly because he never thought he'd find someone who loved him. It never occurred to him it would just happen.

Damn.

Did he tell her? What if she didn't love him?

What if she did?

"Isaac?" Maggie asked, looking at him closely. "Are you okay? You know that was a joke, right? I'm not going anywhere."

"No, it's not that." He led her to a couch, and they both sat down. "I'll tell you about it later." Much later. "Now before you draft that email, I have a question for you."

"What's that?"

"Should the two of us make a couple's basket for the benefit, Margaret?"

Her eyes laughed at him. He knew they were. "You didn't think I'd let you get away with doing anything else, did you, Seven-Thirty?"

IT RAINED the entire afternoon the day of the benefit but not once did Isaac see or hear Maggie act worried. "This is why you booked an inside venue," he overheard her telling Barbara on the phone. "No one will care if it's raining."

Frankly, he didn't think anything short of the apocalypse would keep people away. Barbara had been right, apparently the benefit was *the* event to be at for the weekend. Even people who previously had no interest in anything related to food were comparing basket items.

He'd always attended these things out of a sense of obligation but tonight he was excited and ready to see Maggie shine in the light of her well deserved success. And since he was hosting, he would see it up close.

Because she wanted to get to the venue early, he'd told her he'd pick her up at four-thirty. "That plus three hours is my most favorite time of day," she'd whispered in reply.

He smiled remembering how husky her voice had sounded when she said those words. Hell, it was his most favorite time of day as well. Currently, he waited in the lobby of her building. The doorman had called her apartment when he arrived, but she'd said there was no reason for him to come up because she was heading down at that very moment.

The elevator doors slid open, and she stepped

out, looking like a siren in an ice blue and silver gown. It hugged every curve she had, and he was thankful she'd made the call for him to wait down here. Had he walked into her apartment with her looking the way she did, they would not have been early to the benefit. They would have been lucky to arrive on time.

He walked toward her, bending to give her a kiss much too chaste for his liking. "You look incredible," he whispered as they headed out of the lobby.

Her eyes glowed at his praise and her cheeks flushed a light pink. "Thanks," she said. "I decided not to wear black because doing what everyone else does is boring."

He laughed thinking that would be a great life motto for her. "I like the way you think." He held out his arm. "Shall we?"

She giggled, but took him up on his offer with a confident, "We shall."

Thankfully, the rain had stopped, so he didn't have to let go of her and get his umbrella open. On the way to his car, he passed by a woman he was almost positive he'd passed earlier on his way inside. But Maggie was chatting away about a last minute change she'd made to their basket and how glad she was Isaac had arranged for it to be delivered to the venue, and he promptly forgot all about the woman.

HOURS LATER, near the end of the cocktail hour, the benefit was already a success. Not too bad considering the silent auction for the food baskets wouldn't end for another half hour. He regretted agreeing to host the benefit because his duties allowed him precious little time to spend with Maggie.

Though he wasn't sure she'd noticed. Every time he spotted her, Barbara was introducing her to someone else. The last time he saw her, the duo had been talking with a lady who served on the scholarship board Barbara headed. With a start, he realized that had been almost forty-five minutes ago.

He scanned the crowd for Maggie, thankful for his position on the stage that afforded him a bird's-eye view of the venue. Why couldn't he find her? It should be easy with the gown she wore. Seconds later, he found Barbara talking with a man he didn't recognize, but she was alone. He didn't see Maggie anywhere nearby.

It wasn't a big deal, or at least that's what he tried to tell himself, even as he stepped down from the stage, and made his way to Barbara.

"Isaac," she said. "Can you believe this turnout? We're going to break records tonight. All thanks to Maggie. She's something special."

"Yes, she is," he agreed. "Do you know where she is? I can't find her anywhere."

"She forgot some old stock certificates she wanted to donate tonight and went back to her place to pick them up. I told her it could wait until Monday, but she wanted them to be part of the total we announce tonight, and well, you know how hard-headed she is when her mind's made up. She didn't want to bother you so she took a cab."

"She took a cab back to her apartment." He repeated. "For stock certificates."

"Yes. Don't look so worried. She'll be back soon, I'm sure."

He couldn't shake the feeling something was wrong and sent her a text. She usually replied back right away, but several minutes went by and nothing. "How long ago did she leave?" He pulled up her contact information and called.

"Gracious, Isaac. Calm down."

He took a deep breath, hoping that would convince his heart to slow down, but the phone line rang and rang. "How long ago?" He repeated.

"I don't know. Forty-five minutes? An hour?"

"I need to go. Can you find someone to cover for me?"

Barbara looked worried for the first time since he'd approached her minutes ago. "Is she okay? What's wrong?"

"I'm not sure. Probably nothing, but I'll text you as soon as she's safe in my arms."

Barbara nodded. "Keep her safe. Promise me."

"I will," he vowed even though he had a strange feeling the entire situation was out of his control.

He left immediately, walking with long strides to cover the distance to his car, and then breaking every speed limit in his rush to get to her apartment. The entire time trying not to dwell on the fact that the last time he had this feeling was the day his parents died in a car accident.

MAGGIE SENSED something was off the second she stepped into her apartment. Nothing looked out of place, there were no signs of anyone entering, rather it was an overall feeling of wrong.

That was silly, though, wasn't it? How could her apartment feel wrong? She'd lived here, alone, for years. It was nothing more than her overactive imagination and the romantic suspense novel she'd read the night before. Or the scary movie she watched with Isaac last weekend.

She only needed to get the stock certificates. They were in her bedroom by the door. Placed there so she wouldn't forget them. For all the good it did. It would take ten seconds or less for her to walk down the hall, grab them, and leave. Maybe less. In three minutes, she'd be in a cab, headed back to Isaac.

But the feeling of wrong grew stronger with every step she took in that direction. Deciding it'd be better to get them later, preferably with Isaac with her, she turned to head back out her door and froze.

Her mother-in-law stood in the way, with a gun pointed in her direction.

CHAPTER NINETEEN

"EDITH," Maggie said as calmly as possible, holding her hands up in the air. "What are you doing in my apartment?" She didn't think for a second the woman hated her enough to kill her. Yet, it was hard to come up with how she could think that when the w0man in question held her at gunpoint.

"No, the real question is, why are you here?" Her mother-in-law was dressed in all black, including a black knit hat that covered every strand of her fake, paid for hair, looking like every cat burglar Maggie had ever seen in the movies.

"I fail to see how that's the real question since we're standing in *my* apartment."

"You're always quick with a smart ass reply, aren't you? Do you that's cute?"

At the moment, she thought it was a delay tactic, since Edith was talking and not shooting but she wasn't about to tell her that. Especially since with each passing second, Maggie doubted her initial assessment of Edith's intention not to shoot her more and more.

"No, I don't think it's cute," Maggie answered. "I think it's a legitimate question since my name is on the lease."

"You're supposed to be at that ridiculous benefit on the arm of your boyfriend with the big dick."

Maggie wasn't talking about Isaac's dick with anyone, and that included Edith. "I forgot something and came back to get it."

"You always had a way of screwing everything up, didn't you?" Edith laughed at that. "They say some things never change, but I'm going to prove them wrong tonight. You won't fuck up my plan tonight. Tonight, I'll do it right."

"Do what right?"

"Kill you, of course."

"Wait." Maggie's heart pounded harder and sweat dotted her forehead. There was something Edith said... Maggie repeated her words in her head. "Have you tried to kill me before and got it wrong?"

"Shut up!" Edith waved the gun at her. "I don't want to talk about it."

A few of the puzzle pieces surrounding the house fire slipped into place. How had a brand new house burned to the ground because of faulty wiring? She thought back to that day. It'd been so painful, she'd closed the door on it and vowed never to open it, but now she did.

ELLIS WASN'T SUPPOSED to be at home that night. His father had called a meeting and told Ellis his attendance was mandatory. But Ellis decided to blow the meeting off and went golfing instead. Maggie, not wanting to spend the evening alone, had called and made dinner plans with a few friends.

Tobias had been livid with his son and threatened to disinherit him if he didn't show up. She remembered because Ellis called her on his way to the house to shower and change, telling her that he'd had enough, and tonight he was telling his father off. It was something he'd said before and never done. She didn't expect that time to be any different.

Except it was because Ellis never made it to the meeting. He died soon after arriving home, when the house blew up around him.

. . .

"It was you," Maggie whispered. "You killed Ellis."

With those words, Edith broke. "No, it was an accident! He wasn't supposed to be home." Tears rolled down her face. "It was supposed to be you. Except you weren't there and he was because Tobias made him go to that damn meeting."

If Maggie had any doubt she was dealing with someone who was very sick, the abrupt switching of moods would have erased it all. How long had she been this unstable and did Tobias have any idea?

Edith still clutched the gun but lowered it a touch. Maggie glanced at the door, she hadn't locked it when she came in because she'd only planned on being inside for seconds. She tried to calculate the odds of getting to it without being shot and they weren't in her favor.

Damn it. She was going to have to make a play for the gun. Maggie took a step toward her.

"No!" Edith waved the gun. "Don't come near me, I'll shoot."

Maggie took a step closer. "I don't think you will because if you shoot me, the police won't believe whatever accidental death you've set up here." And what had she set up? How quickly did they need to get out?

Edith sighed. "I can't get your life insurance if you're shot, either."

Thank goodness for small miracles was quickly followed by, *What life insurance?* Probably for the best not to ask her that at the moment, Maggie decided. There would be time to find out what the hell Edith meant if she made it out of this apartment alive. She shuddered at her own words. There would be time to find out what the hell Edith meant *when* she made it out of this apartment alive.

Remembering the time she played with Isaac and she'd been able to relax even though he had used an anal plug on her, she tried to get into the same mind frame. She had to calm her mind down so she could focus on getting out of this nightmare alive.

Unfortunately, she couldn't get her mind to stop racing, though she must have been making some interesting facial expressions because Edith asked her, "What are you doing with your face?"

"It's an exercise I read about recently, it's supposed to counteract anything you do that produces wrinkles so your skin is smoother as you age."

Edith studied her silently and Maggie tried to

make herself look as innocent as possible, but apparently it wasn't a look she could successfully carry off when stressed. Edith gave her a scary smile, tilted her head and said, "I don't believe you."

Maggie acted like it was no big thing. "I don't care whether you do or not." What she cared about was getting out of her apartment and getting out as quickly as possible. Edith wasn't stable and there was no telling how much longer she'd be able to halfway reason with the woman.

Her cell phone was in her purse, which she'd placed on the foyer table beside the front door. Of course Edith had to pick tonight when there was no way for her to carry her phone in her pocket the way she did ninety-nine percent of the time. Now it looked as if she had to decide between finding a way to get to the door or to her purse. Neither of which appeared workable at the moment.

The box near the front door buzzed. Edith kept the barrel of the gun aimed at Maggie.

Maggie tried to keep her voice calm. "It's the doorman. He knows I'm here. I have to answer." Not only that, but the box was near the door. If she could answer the box, it was possible she could open the door.

"I'll work the box. You can talk to him from

there." Edith walked two steps backward, somehow keeping the gun aimed at Maggie.

Damn it. What she wouldn't give to have Isaac's ability to poker face at the moment.

The box buzzed again.

"Don't try anything cute," Edith said, and pressed the answer button.

Why? You already said you can't shoot me. Maggie wanted to ask, but bit her tongue because she only saw madness in Edith's eyes and there was no predicting how she might react. "Yes?" she asked, hoping she'd projected enough, and the doorman heard her.

"Good evening, Ms. Warren," the doorman said. "I wanted to let you know that Mr. Tobias Warren is on his way up."

"What?" Maggie replied but Edith had already disconnected. She was screwed. While she may have had a chance against Edith, there was no way she'd be able to fight Tobias. The doorman had done all he could in letting her know the man was on the way. He couldn't have stopped him because Tobias owned the place.

The only thing providing her any comfort was the perplexed look on Edith's face.

"Wh… wh… why is he here?" she asked.

It took too much brain power to figure out the answer to that question, and besides Maggie knew she more than likely didn't want to know.

Someone knocked on the door. "Edith!" Tobias called. "Open up, baby."

"Toby?" With that one word, her voice changed, and though she looked like a dangerous adult, she sounded almost childlike.

"I'm here, baby," Tobias said. "Open the door and let me help."

Edith's eyes grew large. "You will?"

"Of course. I'll always help my girl."

Please, God, Maggie prayed. *Please let him know his wife is sick.* She only hoped that somehow Tobias meant he'd help his wife get treatment and not help kill his daughter-in-law. She hated having to place her hope in him, and she glanced around the room looking for anything she could use as a weapon. Her eyes fell on a letter opener on a table near the door. It had been a wedding present, and was gaudy, but it was heavy and sharp, so they'd kept it.

"Door's unlocked," she told Edith.

As soon as Edith turned to open the door, Maggie leaped in front of the mail table, grabbing the letter opener, and hiding it behind her back. She watched in shock as Tobias gently took Edith in his arms, while taking the gun out of her hands.

He looked at Maggie and for a split second she thought he'd aim it right back at her. But he called over his shoulder, "I've got her. She's disarmed."

"Toby?" Edith asked in that childlike voice as several muscular men stormed into the apartment. "Toby?" She called again as they restrained her.

"Maggie? Oh my, God. Are you okay?"

"Isaac?"

He made it to her before she could blink and then she was in his arms and nothing else mattered.

CHAPTER TWENTY

It was nearly dawn by the time they made it to Isaac's penthouse. Even then he'd almost had to resort to threatening bodily injury because people kept wanting to question Maggie.

He carried her into his bedroom and put her on the bed. She still had on her ice blue gown, and though she had to be exhausted, he knew she wouldn't be able to sleep yet.

"I can't believe Edith killed Ellis," she said. "Accidental or not. And I can't believe you came after me. How did you know?"

She'd already asked him that at least five times and his answer never changed. "I just knew."

When he rushed into the lobby of her building and found it swarming with police officers, firemen, and various medical personnel, he feared he was too late. But then he'd spotted Tobias talking with several people at the front desk. It took everything he had not to punch the man, but to ask him in a not-so-polite voice what the fuck was going on.

"And how did Tobias not know how sick and delusional his wife was?" Maggie asked.

"Good question."

Isaac still had trouble understanding the entire story himself. But from what he could piece together, Edith and been ill for a long time, and Tobias, busy with his company and making an even bigger name for himself, was rarely around her. He claimed ignorance on the letter Edith sent Maggie and the chef contract that nearly ruined the benefit.

"At least he was observant enough to notice she was up to something tonight and followed her," Maggie said.

"Only because she wasn't able to get to the wiring of the apartment like she was the house, and went back to the house to get Tobias's gun." The only reason Tobias was still breathing was because the gun had been unloaded. When he thought…. Isaac shook his head refusing to allow his thoughts to go down that path. He held out his hand. "Come here and let me help you get that gown off. You can't be comfortable."

He was as gentle as possible preparing Maggie for bed. It was difficult when what he really wanted to do was hold her to him as tight as possible. She yawned once he'd washed her as best he could with a washcloth and warm water and slipped a soft cotton gown over her head. He tucked her into bed, stripped down to his underwear, and climbed in beside her.

She curved her body as close as possible to his and he stroked her back, breathing her in. They'd already agreed she'd be moving in with him. It was a new chapter of his life and he couldn't wait to write it with her.

"I love you, Seven-Thirty," she said, eyes closed but with a heartwarming grin. "Even though you're a control freak."

"I love you, too." He kissed her forehead and laughed. "Even though you're nothing but chaos."

EPILOGUE

ONE MONTH Later

MAGGIE JOGGED up the steps of the brownstone on West 70th Street after checking to make sure she had the correct address. She was rarely late anymore, but was cutting it close at the moment. It would have been possible to blame her almost lateness on Barbara, but the truth was she'd been just as wrapped up in work as her boss. Especially since the work she'd been doing was planning an engagement party for Barbara's grandson Lance and his now-finance, Celeste.

Lance had called Barbara earlier in the day to let her know of the engagement, as well as to tell her he and Celeste would be coming home at the end of September when Celeste's term with the summer orchestra ended. She had a new position lined up, but it wouldn't start until November, so they were coming back to the States for a month.

She rang the doorbell and took a step back expecting the real estate agent to answer and was pleasantly surprised when Isaac answered.

"Hey, you," she said giving him a quick kiss as she stepped inside. "Where's Dana?"

"She had a child emergency and had to run off. She said for us to look around and lock up. I'll have someone drop off the keys tomorrow."

When they'd decided to live together, Maggie had told him in no uncertain terms she did not want to stay in her apartment. They'd both agreed his penthouse was too impersonal, and when the real estate agent they hired suggested brownstones, they'd been intrigued. Unfortunately, this was the fifth one they'd seen, having been unimpressed with the first four. All four had been lovely homes, but renovated so extensively it was barbaric.

"There's a difference between renovation and restoration," she'd told Isaac when their agent couldn't believe they weren't interested in the fourth property she showed them. "Not one place we've seen reflects that knowledge."

"What do you think of this one?'" Maggie asked him.

"I've only seen this room," he replied. "I was waiting for you before taking the grand tour."

"Let's not wait another second," she said, grabbing his hand. "We'll see if the fifth time is the charm."

Isaac snorted and followed her into the hallway. Maggie came to a sudden stop in front of a staircase, not sure she believed her eyes.

"Is that mahogany?" she asked in a whisper. She dropped his hand and stroked a banister. "Do you think it's original?"

Isaac studied the wood. "Looks like mahogany to me and if I had to guess, I'd say it's original to the property." He typed something in his phone. "I'll make a note to ask Dana."

"I have a good feeling about this one," she said. "Anyone who put that much time and effort into a banister won't skimp out on the rest of the house."

Thirty minutes later, she was thrilled with how right she'd been. There were original touches throughout the home, including a Tiffany window and additional woodworks of cherry and oak.

"I can't decide if I like the private garden or the master bedroom library the best," she shared with Isaac after they left and were walking to his car.

"Hate to break it to you, but you're flat out crazy if you think you'll be *reading* in the master bedroom. Besides, I was thinking it'd make much more sense to set that area apart for play. After all, it is in the master bedroom."

His sense of humor was so dry, she often couldn't tell if he was joking or not. All she could think to say was, "Really?"

"Absolutely. The built-in bookcase will be perfect for storing sex toys."

Maybe he wasn't joking.

By the time they made it to Isaac's penthouse, they'd already called Dana and made an offer for the brownstone.

"I can't believe we found a house. I'd almost given up," she told Isaac as his elevator doors slid open. She took a step out of the elevator and stopped. White lights had been strung up and around in what she finally saw was a pathway. "What is this?"

Isaac didn't answer. He took her hand and led her down the illuminated path which came to a stop at the doors leading to his outside room. He let go her long enough to open the doors, then he took her hand again, and they stepped outside.

The white lights continued outside, strung around the climbing plants and creating a fairy tale setting. She turned toward Isaac and found him watching her. Unlike times in the past, she read every emotion present in his expression: joy, love, desire. They were all there, and their intensity burned into her soul because they represented what he felt for her.

"I had no way of knowing when I planned this that it would follow us making an offer for what will become our home." He glanced over her shoulder and laughed. "I didn't plan for the time of day, either."

She didn't have to look at the clock behind her to know exactly what time it was.

"I never planned to fall in love, and the last few months since we've met have been the happiest of my life. And, I know you're not there yet, but I plan on marrying you someday. I can be patient as long as you know my desired outcome."

She did. They spoke of it often, and she planned on marrying him, too.

"But I want to ask this of you now." He reached into his inside jacket pocket and pulled out a light blue slender box. He lifted the lid revealing a delicate silver chain with an o-ring. "Margaret, will you wear my collar?"

Isaac may have never planned to fall in love, but she never planned for anyone to offer her a collar. And just as he jumped in head first, she wanted to do likewise.

"Yes, Sir, Seven-Thirty." She slid to her knees before him and blinked her happy tears back. "I will proudly wear your collar."

"Thank you." His strong hands came to her neck, and he clasped the chain into place. "Let me see," he said, pulling her to her feet. She lifted her chin, proud to show it off. His eyes flashed. "You make me so happy. I'm a fortunate man, to have you with me, to be building a life with you. And I can't wait until we move into our new place because I plan to fuck you in every room."

Her body temperature went up twenty degrees just thinking about it. "That's a lot of rooms, Sir," she teased.

He shifted his body so she felt his erection. "I'm up for it, are you?"

"Yes, Sir. Very. Just one more thing." She bit her bottom lip. "You don't really plan on putting sex toys on the bookshelf, do you?"

He raised an eyebrow which told her not a damn thing and then laughed at the scowl she gave him. "I hadn't planned to, I was teasing," he said. "But now? Hell fucking, yes."

She couldn't help it, she laughed right along with him, because who would have thought Isaac Gregory would ever have a bookshelf filled with sex toys?

DON'T MISS

FOK

Wall Street Royals, Book One

"...so damn HOT and intense, what an amazing start
to a series..." -The Sassy Nerd Review

229

FOK

CHAPTER ONE

In her mind, Celeste Walsh was a badass. She never backed down, never averted her gaze first, and never took shit from anyone.

In reality, however, though she refused to be a doormat, she had yet to blossom into full-blown badassery. The closest she'd been able to get was to perfect the art of remaining utterly calm in the face of anything. Her roommate, Reagan, told her it was her superpower. Celeste had snorted and said if that was true, she wanted to exchange it for something useful, like mind reading or invisibility.

Although, she had to admit that today this odd superpower could come in handy. She was auditioning for a scholarship, but that wasn't anything new. In fact, this was her eleventh scholarship audition. What made this audition different was that it would be the last. Last audition. Her last hope.

If she didn't score this scholarship, she wouldn't be attending Juilliard in the fall. Which would also mean no longer being able to stay in New York. She'd be on a bus headed back home to Middle-of-Nowhere Virginia. Upon arrival, her parents would put her to work, either washing dishes or bussing tables at the family's farm to table restaurant.

She shivered, determined to get this one.

"Hey, Celeste," one of her fellow applicants, Erin, said.

Celeste smiled and greeted the young woman in a similar financial situation as her own. They'd auditioned at many of the same scholarships and had received rejections from the same ones. There were a few they hadn't heard from yet.

"Did you hear?" Erin asked, her eyes dancing the way they did when she wanted to share the latest juicy gossip.

"Probably not." Celeste rarely listened to gossip or watched the news. Her life revolved around the violin. Violin. School. Violin. She possessed little time for anything else in her life. And she didn't apologize or make excuses for it. Especially with the new piece she planned for today's audition.

"Barbara Murphy is in the hospital," Erin said.

"Really?" Celeste asked. That wasn't gossip. Barbara Murphy headed and funded the scholarship they were auditioning for today, in memory of her daughter. Melinda Murphy had been a pianist and had also attended Juilliard years ago when she was younger. She'd died young, but Celeste wasn't sure if she'd ever heard how. "Who's running the audition?"

"No one I've talked with knows."

They both turned to look at the auditorium doors. The first group to audition, vocalists, had entered only five minutes ago. It wasn't long before the doors opened and three guys walked out.

"Fucking asshole," the tallest one said and the other two nodded and murmured in agreement.

"Who's running the audition with Mrs. Murphy in the hospital?" Someone nearby asked.

"Her grandson," the tall guy answered. "Some Wall Street hotshot who doesn't know shit about the arts."

The trio of vocalists left amid a growing rumble of discontent. A discontent that, unfortunately, remained in their wake. However, Celeste felt no need to continue talking about the grandson she couldn't do anything about. She retreated to her corner of the room and tried to tune out the noise around her like she always did, by picturing herself playing the violin.

Knowing this was her last audition and one of the largest scholarships offered, she'd changed her audition piece. The composer wasn't as well know as the ones her competition would play, nor was the piece itself known by very many outside the music world. If this grandson was as clueless as the vocalist had alluded to, should she play something more well known?

She forced herself to breathe deep and calm. As she did, the music she needed to play made itself known. When a harried assistant called for her group, Celeste rose from her seat, lost in the calm, ready to play, and with no worries about a grandson who may or may not know the difference between a violin and a cello.

Lance Braxton cut the violinist off after nine seconds of playing. "That's enough. Next!"

Beside him, his grandmother's personal assistant, Richard, sighed and signaled for a ten minute break. Lance raised an eyebrow at him, and Richard took a deep breath before turning to address the man at his side. "Mr. Braxton, you can't cut them off like that. You must allow them to finish playing."

Lance placed his pen on the table, so it lined up exactly parallel to the pad it was next to. Only when he was certain it rested precisely where he wanted, did he turn to the man his grandmother said she couldn't operate without. "Richard," he said slowly, as if gathering his thoughts. Which he wasn't. "Perhaps you have nothing better to do today than to sit here and listen to Tchaikovsky over and over, but some of us have actual work to do."

Richard opened his mouth as if he would interrupt, but Lance shot him a look that made him change his mind. "You have worked for my grandmother for three years; however, I have been her grandson for much longer. Do you understand?"

Richard was smart enough to only nod.

"Though I do not typically sit here and listen, I know the characteristics my grandmother requires for the recipient of the scholarship bearing my mother's name. Therefore, if I determine an applicant has none of these characteristics, I'm doing us all a favor by not wasting time and letting that person go."

Lance estimated Richard cost him valuable time by putting him in a position to explain himself. He rarely explained himself. Even rarer did he do so to anyone's personal assistant. The fact he'd just done so, and that there were people who could hear the conversation, irritated him. He needed to move this thing along. He had real work to do. Though he couldn't deny his grandmother's request when she asked him to take her place today. His Grandmother Murphy was the one person he couldn't tell no.

Beside him, Richard swallowed and sweat beaded on his forehead. "Yes, Mr. Braxton. I understand."

Lance nodded. "You're excused. I'll finish up here."

The other man scrambled to pick up his notebook and pens. Lance waited with a patience he didn't feel until the door closed behind the assistant his grandmother insisted was a lifesaver. He didn't see how, but Richard wasn't his problem. At least on most days. Today, he'd been a major pain in the ass.

"Let's go, people," he said to no one in particular, knowing someone would hear and usher out the next applicant. He shuffled the papers in front of him. How many more did he have to sit through?

The click of heels on the stage alerted him the next applicant was in place. He pulled the information sheet he had on whoever it was. "Name?" He asked without looking up.

"Celeste Walsh."

Her voice was delicate and feminine. Yet something in her tone spoke of a quietly held strength. It intrigued him and he looked up. She was stunning for lack of a better word. At some point her dark hair had been pulled up, now, however, more than a few strands had fallen free, giving her a wild and untamed appearance.

An appearance that should have been at odds with her elegant yet subtle black floor length dress, but somehow wasn't. In fact, her entire ensemble could be described as a hot mess. Instead she was one of the hottest women he'd seen in a long time.

She stood waiting, the very epitome of calm, violin in hand as if she had all the time in the world. Not at all as if he held her future in his hands, which he did based upon the paper in front of him.

He wanted to crush the paper. Because in doing so he would have no ties to the glorious creature before him. Which meant he could do any damn thing she would allow him to do to her. And he'd make sure she wanted the same things he did.

But he couldn't do that, so he cleared his throat and said, "Whenever you're ready, Ms. Walsh."

She gave him a curt nod, closed her eyes, and played.

He recognized the song within the first few bars, and it both impressed and surprised him. He should stop her. It was a difficult and complex piece, even for the most accomplished violinist, and he didn't want to listen while she fucked up her chance at his scholarship. Yet, he couldn't because that moment in time served one purpose - for Celeste Walsh to play her violin for him.

Not that he thought for a second he might stop her. He couldn't. Not with the way she played. With Celeste, playing violin involved her entire body. She swayed at times. Others, she held still. No matter what, though, her face was a myriad of expressions while she held the bow and touched the strings as she would a lover.

She kept her eyes closed the entire time, and Lance felt as if he were peeking at a private or intimate moment. Her performance was one of the most erotic things he'd ever witnessed. In fact, music had never aroused him the way it did when she played. Never had he been so thankful for a table. He'd hate for her, or anyone for that matter, to see the erection her playing caused.

He wondered if anyone else had offered her a scholarship and this audition was just for fun? Had such passion filled all of her pervious auditions? Was she always so euphoric while she played? It was borderline obscene, and he loved it. He wanted more of it.

He wanted her.

She held him captive until the last note sounded and even when its echo had disappeared from the room, she held still, not yet releasing him from her spell. Until she moved, he didn't breathe.

Finally, she opened one eye and then the other, looking around almost as if she'd forgotten where she was. That wasn't possible, though, was it? She looked toward where he sat, the room's lighting did not allow her to see him, and for a second looked as if he'd caught her doing something naughty.

Holy hell. Did she get turned on playing the violin? He didn't know, but damn it all to hell, he would find out.

She remained on stage, clearly expecting him to dismiss her. He didn't feel bad in the least keeping her waiting. Her feet shifted the slightest bit. The small movement was so far the only hint she wasn't near as calm as she portrayed.

He picked up a paper from the pile in front of him and made it a point not to look at her when he spoke. "You're twenty-five?"

"Yes, sir."

Her unexpected use of 'sir' sent a shock throughout his body. He opened his mouth to tell her she didn't have to call him 'sir' but shut it just as quickly because he'd have added "Yet."

He kept his gaze even and uninterested when he lifted his head. "You're significantly older than most of your peers auditioning today."

She remained silent, and he nodded in approval. Yes, she would be a fun one. "Why are you only now applying to Juilliard?" he asked.

"After I graduated from high school, my grandmother came to live with us. My mom couldn't both watch her and do what she had been doing with the family business. I took over my Mom's role so she could care for her mother."

"What was your mother's job?"

"She was the pastry chef at our family's restaurant."

Impressive and not listed on her application. "You worked as a pastry chef for seven years?"

"I wasn't always the pastry chef. Sometimes I waited tables and sometimes I washed dishes."

He nodded, not interested in the past, and definitely not interested in listening about her washing dishes. "Why the violin? Why now?"

She shifted her gaze to somewhere beyond him,

and her eyes took on a faraway look. "Because it's my time now. My time to stand on my own and to make something of myself. Because I love the violin and nothing would make me happier than to play it every day. And because I don't want to work in a restaurant all my life."

And she shouldn't, he thought. Not with the way she'd just played that piece. Working in a restaurant would waste her talent, and he couldn't allow that to happen. Not when he had a way to ensure it wouldn't.

He stacked the pile of papers in front of him and tapped them on the table. What was the name of the woman working on stage who ushered the applicants on and off? She'd introduced herself when he'd first arrived, but he hadn't made note of it, deciding it was a detail Richard could worry with. Which did him no good since he gave the man the boot.

"Thank you, Ms. Walsh," he said to the waiting woman on stage and smiled inwardly at the curt nod she gave in response and how she turned to walk away as if he'd excused her. "I did not say I excused you."

She froze and turned. "But you said -"

"Do not make it a habit to repeat back to me what I said. I have no trouble remembering my words, especially if I spoke them mere seconds before. What I said was, 'Thank you, Ms. Walsh' which in no way sounds like, 'You are excused.' Now, move back to where you were."

While she took the few necessary steps to return to her initial spot in the middle of the stage, he addressed those still waiting and the woman whose name he couldn't remember. "That's all for this year. Thank you for coming. You're excused." Ignoring the muttered protests, he turned his attention back to Celeste. "See how that works? The 'you're excused' part?"

She gaped at him in shock though. Probably wasn't hearing anything at all. From the look on her face, everything he said went in one ear and straight out the other. He didn't say anything else to her. Best she learn from the start how he operated.

The woman with the name he couldn't remember stepped out the shadows and onto the stage. She held one hand like a shield over her eyes, probably trying to see him better. "Mr. Braxton?"

"Yes." He knew what she would say, and he didn't want to hear it. After gathering together the few things he'd brought in, he walked to the stage.

As expected, as soon as his foot hit the first step, she appeared before him, flustered and flipping through pages on a clipboard. "There are three more violinists waiting backstage, and we haven't even started the brass group and...." Her voice trailed off when she looked up and saw him shaking his head.

"No," he said.

"No?"

"There will be no more auditions for this year's scholarship." Having made his way up the stairs to the stage, he turned to Celeste. "Get your things together and come with me."

OUT NOW

AMERICAN ASSHOLE

"Scorching sex, well-developed characters, occasional bursts of humor, and skillful plotting make Me's series launch a must-read." - PUBLISHERS WEEKLY

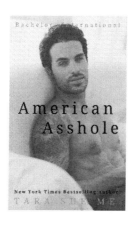

He groaned my name as he pressed deeper inside me and I fisted the white sheets so tightly my knuckles almost matched their color.

We shouldn't be doing this, but more importantly *I* shouldn't be doing this. I should have never let it get this far. I knew better.

I should have never said yes to dinner. I should have never said yes to this trip. I should have never said yes to the contract.
But damn it all I had, even knowing what it would cost us both.

His weight pressed me into the mattress and his breath was hot in my ear. "Are you still with me?" Then for good measure he shifted his hips so his next thrust hit a new spot inside me and I moaned in pleasure.

It seemed I was unable to say no to the man. Nor did I want to. My body moved with his, desperate to draw him deeper.

"Are you?" he asked again, his lips brushing my nape and sending shivers down my spine.

"Yes. Oh, God, yes."

Headmaster

BACHELOR INTERNATIONAL:

American Asshole

THE DATE DUO:

The Date Dare

The Date Deal

WALL STREET ROYALS:

FOK

OTHERS:

Her Last Hello

Altered Allies (currently unavailable)

Writing as Tara Thomas

Shattered Fear*

Hidden Fate*

Twisted End*

Darkest Night

Deadly Secret

Broken Promise

*eNovella

ABOUT THE AUTHOR

Even though she graduated with a degree in science, Tara knew she'd never be happy doing anything other than writing. Specifically, writing love stories.

She started with a racy BDSM story and found she was not quite prepared for the unforeseen impact it would have. Nonetheless, she continued and The Submissive Series novels would go on to be both *New York Times* and *USA Today* Bestsellers. One of those, THE MASTER, was a 2017 RITA finalist for Best Erotic Romance. Well over one million copies of her books have been sold worldwide.

www.tarasueme.com

60366261R10154

Made in the USA
Middletown, DE
15 August 2019